Readers love the Bronco's Boys series by ANDREW GREY

Inside Out

"I knew I had to read this as soon as I saw the cover, and I was not disappointed."

—Hearts on Fire

Upside Down

"I loved this book."

—It's About The Book

Backward

"*Backward* is a well-crafted addition to this series… I do believe this is my favorite Andrew Grey series now…"

—The Novel Approach

Round and Round

"…this book offered mystery, romance, friendship and a great group of characters."

—Inked Rainbow Reads

Over and Back

"Well done, Andrew Grey, for yet another love story that's a little bit dark, a little bit angsty and a whole lot of fun to read."

—Love Bytes

More priase for
ANDREW GREY

Twice Baked

"This a great second chance romance novel... There is loads of charm and romance."

—MM Good Book Reviews

"I love it when a story can cause me to keep guessing until end and make it plausible at the same time. Very well done."

—Gay Book Reviews

Heartward

"Whoooo. This one hits you right in the feels. Man."

—Love Bytes

"Not only is it a book about finding a home but it is a book about finding a family. Andrew Grey did a great job on this book. It is happy, sad, mysterious, and second chances at having it all. I really love books like this."

—Gay Book Reviews

Pulling Strings

"I don't have any problem recommending Pulling Strings. It's a good, solid mystery/romance, and if that's up your alley, you should definitely pick this one up."

—Joyfully Jay

"Once again I am in awe of Mr. Grey's ability to write about so many different subjects..."

—Paranormal Romance Guild

By Andrew Grey

Accompanied by a Waltz
All for You
Between Loathing and Love
Borrowed Heart
Buried Passions
Chasing the Dream
Crossing Divides
Dominant Chord
Dutch Treat
Eastern Cowboy
Heartward
In Search of a Story
New Tricks
Noble Intentions
North to the Future
One Good Deed
On Shaky Ground
The Playmaker
Pulling Strings
Rebound
Reunited
Running to You
Saving Faithless Creek
Shared Revelations
Survive and Conquer
Three Fates
To Have, Hold, and Let Go
Turning the Page
Twice Baked
Unfamiliar Waters
Whipped Cream

ART
Legal Artistry • Artistic Appeal
Artistic Pursuits • Legal Tender

BOTTLED UP
The Best Revenge • Bottled Up
Uncorked • An Unexpected Vintage

BRONCO'S BOYS
Inside Out • Upside Down
Backward • Round and Round
Over and Back • Above and Beyond

THE BULLRIDERS
A Wild Ride • A Daring Ride
A Courageous Ride

BY FIRE
Redemption by Fire
Strengthened by Fire
Burnished by Fire • Heat Under Fire

CARLISLE COPS
Fire and Water • Fire and Ice
Fire and Rain
Fire and Snow • Fire and Hail
Fire and Fog

CARLISLE DEPUTIES
Fire and Flint • Fire and Granite
Fire and Agate • Fire and Obsidian
Fire and Onyx

CHEMISTRY
Organic Chemistry • Biochemistry
Electrochemistry
Chemistry Anthology

DREAMSPUN DESIRES
The Lone Rancher
Poppy's Secret
The Best Worst Honeymoon Ever

EYES OF LOVE
Eyes Only for Me • Eyes Only for You

FOREVER YOURS
Can't Live Without You
Never Let You Go

Published by Dreamspinner Press
www.dreamspinnerpresss.com

Published by DREAMSPINNER PRESS
www.dreamspinnerpresss.com

ABOVE
AND
BEYOND
ANDREW GREY

Published by

DREAMSPINNER PRESS

5032 Capital Circle SW, Suite 2, PMB# 279, Tallahassee, FL 32305-7886 USA
www.dreamspinnerpress.com

Above and Beyond
© 2020 Andrew Grey

Cover Art
© 2020 L.C. Chase
http://www.lcchase.com
Cover content is for illustrative purposes only and any person depicted on the cover is a model.

Trade Paperback ISBN: 978-1-64405-368-3
Digital ISBN: 978-1-64405-262-4
Library of Congress Control Number: 2019955047
Trade Paperback published March 2020
v. 1.0

Printed in the United States of America
∞
This paper meets the requirements of
ANSI/NISO Z39.48-1992 (Permanence of Paper).

To all the fans of this series. It's always difficult to say goodbye.

CHAPTER 1

ELLIOTT HASTINGS glanced toward the front door of the club for the hundredth time in about three hours. He needed to calm down and get his act together. He took a deep breath, turned, and bumped into one of the guys hurrying across the floor. Somehow, he managed to not drop the tray of glasses he'd just cleared and was taking back to be washed. That was a God-ordained miracle, considering he'd already spilled a drink and had a martini glass shatter on the concrete floor. Of course, the guys around all clapped, because that's what assholes did when something like that happened. Elliott wondered how people like that actually had graduated from kindergarten.

He got the glasses back to the dish room without breaking any more.

"You need to be more careful," Grant, the head of the waitstaff, told him as he got ready to head out again. "You're here on a trial basis."

Elliott nodded, and his self-esteem took another little ding. He had practically begged for a chance. Elliott needed a job badly or he was going to find that the life he had just managed to start was going to come crashing down around his ears. Leaving everything had been hard, but necessary, though leaving his dog with a friend had nearly killed him. And starting over had been difficult enough, but having to try to do it again when he was barely hanging on by a thread as it was…. "I know, I'm sorry." He grabbed a clean tray and headed to check on his tables.

The beat of the music hit him like a wall as soon as he passed through the door out of the back area and into the club. Part of him fed off that beat and the energy, while another part would never get used to it. When he was out there, the music largely retreated. But when he left and then came back, it was like he'd just walked into the club for the first time. Still, he put that aside as best he could and returned to work.

1

"Can I get you something from the bar?" Elliott asked a group of six guys who had crammed themselves around the table he had just cleared. It was one of the smaller ones, and the guys were going to find it hard to keep their drinks straight. Maybe they didn't care.

The guy closest to him, wearing a maroon shirt and painted-on jeans, turned in his chair, parting his legs a little, probably to give Elliott a better view. Elliott ignored the move. He'd seen it before, and frankly, he wasn't interested. Grant had told him that this was a job. It didn't matter that he was cute and that the guys in here were all gay—they were customers, and he was expected to act professionally, be polite, smile, and get what they wanted, but he wasn't to flirt or spend extra time talking. Being nice was one thing; trolling for dates was quite another. And Elliott was more than ready to be done with that sort of thing.

"I'd like a martini, sweetheart." The guy flashed a million-watt smile, but Elliott knew what those meant as well.

He jotted down the order and took the rest of them for the table. He turned, and Maroon Shirt patted his backside. Elliott whipped around, glaring and shaking his head at the man before hurrying to fill the orders.

"Did he just grab you?" Hank asked from behind the bar.

"He patted me, yeah. I think I took care of it, though." God, Elliott wished he could get his voice to work. He was getting so tired of being afraid all the time. He felt like some jumpy cat ready to run and hide at any moment.

"If you need any backup, be sure to tell one of us. That sort of thing isn't allowed." Hank crooked his finger and leaned over the bar. "You are a cocktail waiter, not a piece of meat for anyone to decide that they can feel up. This is a job, not a profession." He smiled a little. "Don't be afraid to tell someone about things like that or to ask for help. It's what we're here for."

"I don't want to cause trouble," Elliott said. That was the very last thing he wanted.

"You aren't causing trouble. Someone like Mr. Touchy-Feely over there is the one to borrow trouble. Bull and his other security guys will be more than happy to toss guys like that out on their ears." Hank gave him another smile and filled his drink order. "Go on, and know we have your back."

"Thanks…." Elliott returned to the table, delivered the drinks, and made sure the cash they gave him was enough to cover it.

"Keep the change, little guy," Maroon Shirt said. There was a pretty generous tip included. "And maybe when you go on a break, you can come over and spend a few minutes with us."

"Thank you," Elliott said for the tip and ignored the rest. "Can I bring you anything else?" He almost didn't wait for an answer before heading to his next table, taking away the empties, and getting their orders for refills before making his way to the bar. "It's busy tonight."

Hank nodded, taking care of Elliott's order and putting the dirty glasses in a busser tray for him. "It is Friday, but who knows, maybe somebody put something in the water today."

Elliott rolled his eyes. "Yeah, let's-behave-badly juice." He glanced at the table. "He asked me to stop by on my break."

"Huh…," Hank said. "Look. When it's break time, go over to that table instead and introduce yourselves. The guys are nice. The one looking this way is Bull's husband, and another is Harry's. Those four guys are great, and they aren't going to let anyone hit on you. It will give you a few minutes away from Mr. Grabby Hands to let him cool down." Hank stood up straighter, and Elliott followed his glare across the room to the table with the grabber.

Elliott took his drinks back to the tables and continued making the rounds. That was the part of his job he liked and what he was good at. He had been waiting tables in restaurants and clubs for years. Elliott knew what he was doing. It was the fear that crept into him that made him as jumpy as a cat.

For much of the next hour, he managed to avoid Maroon Shirt's table. He already knew what they wanted and brought them refills, but didn't stay long.

"Hank told me someone has been giving you trouble," Grant said, when Elliott was taking plates and things to the dish room.

"I handled it," Elliott said.

3

"Okay. Just so you know, we have your back." Grant smiled.

At break time, Elliott took Hank's advice and approached the table of guys a year or two older than he was. "Hi," he said nervously. "I'm Elliott. Hank said that I should come over on my break and...." He felt stupid and was about to tell them never mind and scurry back into his little rabbit hole. He could take his break in the office area.

"I'm Zach, and this is Kevin, Tristan, and Jeremy." Zach pushed out the empty chair at the table. "Of course you can join us. Have a seat. Do you need something to drink?"

"I'm working, so a Diet Coke or something."

Jeremy slipped off his stool and wove through the crowd toward the bar.

Elliott sat down and placed his hands in his lap, checking the front door and hating himself for doing so.

"Are you expecting trouble to come storming through?" Zach asked. "You keep looking at the front door with dread. This is a safe place. Yeah, there are a lot of people here, but there's plenty of security. Whatever you're worried about, Bull and the guys can handle."

"Are you here all the time?" Elliott practically had to shout to be heard over the music, and it made his voice rough.

"No. We usually come in a few nights a week," Zach told him. "We work, but with the guys here until all hours most of the week, it's a chance for us to get together and to at least be where our husbands are." Zach smiled as Bull—a huge bald man—approached, leaned down to Zach, and kissed him fully.

"Everything all right?" Bull asked Zach.

"Yeah. Apparently, our new server, Elliott, is having trouble with a table and some wandering hands."

"Geez, word gets around fast." Elliott was determined not to blush because they were talking about him. "I handled it, sir," he told Bull.

Bull turned to face him. "Okay, but we'll keep an eye on them. If they made advances to you, then they might do it to others. We don't allow that kind of troublemaking here. This is a gay club, and we all know that guys come in here to meet other guys and that's part of what we're here for. But we won't stand for anyone being accosted or pawed

4

at when they aren't interested." Bull's gaze grew hard for a second and then softened. "We're a family here. The people who work for us, Harry and I, all of the people here, we look out for them."

Elliott nodded. "Thank you." Those few words were as close to a family as he had right now. He swallowed hard. That was just what he needed to hear at the moment.

Bull placed a hand on Zach's shoulder and leaned closer to say something in his ear. Zach grew red, and Elliott turned away; it seemed like an intrusion to watch. Then they parted, and Elliott's heart ached for something like that. He'd thought he'd found it, but like so many of the things in his life, he'd been wrong about it.

Bull moved away, the huge man giving Elliott a single pat on the shoulder before disappearing into the crowd.

Jeremy returned and distributed a round of glasses for each of them. Elliott tried to hide his heartache by taking a drink of the soda. It went down cold and wet his throat.

Elliott checked the time and saw he had five more minutes. He drank the rest and set the empty glass on the table. "I don't want to intrude on your time together," Elliott said, and went to get up from the chair.

"Dude," Jeremy said, "just sit and stay off your feet for a few minutes. It's okay." He smiled. "Did you just start?"

"Yeah. This is my third day, and already I've broken three glasses and nearly dumped two trays." Elliott felt like such an idiot, knowing he was better than that.

"Why are you so nervous?" Jeremy asked. "Grant only hires experienced servers, so I figure something has to be up." He smiled. "And speak of the devil." He stepped off the chair and hugged Grant as he came to the table.

"Hey, guys," Grant said, and turned to Elliott. "Any more problems?"

"No. But if I have any, I'll come to you or Bull right away." This time Elliott did get up. "I need to get back. Thank you," he said to Jeremy and the other guys, then hurried to get a tray and check on his tables. He was glad that the night was nearly half over.

An hour later, Elliott was making his way around the edge of the club, through a crowd of people watching the dancers writhe and grind to the techno beat, when a hand descended on his shoulder. "You've been busy, little rabbit."

Elliott pulled away and turned around. He hated that name. "And who are you, the big bad wolf?" he retorted, shaking his head. "I'm sorry, but I'm not interested. Now please let me get back to work." Why did guys like this think just because they had nice eyes, good hair, and were built pretty well that they could get away with this kind of behavior?

"Come on, little rabbit. I have a carrot with your name on it."

Elliott couldn't help it. He practically dropped his empty tray as he started laughing. "You have got to be kidding me. Does a line like that really work on anyone? Go back to your friends or else I'll call security and they can take care of you." He turned away and headed toward the bar, but was wheeled around and ended up facing a rather drunk and pissed-off patron in a maroon shirt.

"I've been nice and tipped you well…."

Elliott's eyes widened. "I'm not someone you can buy with a tip and then think you can come on to like this. Go back to your table and leave me alone." He looked around to see if he could find anyone who could help him. When a pair of intense green eyes met his for a second, Elliott's stomach went cold as ice. The crowd shifted, and when Elliott looked again, he didn't see the man he expected. He turned and hurried away, jostling a few people, then slammed into a solid brick wall of muscle. Elliott hadn't seen him before, but the guy was six feet six, at least, and wide as hell.

"Hey, what's wrong?" It was only when he backed away that he saw the guy was dressed in a black polo that stretched across his ample chest, with the Bronco's logo on the left side.

"The guy there wouldn't leave me alone. He grabbed my backside earlier, and now he's pushing his suit. He thinks because he tipped me well that…." The words spilled out even as Elliott kept a watchful eye for the man he feared most of all, but he didn't see him and wondered if his fear was conjuring up things.

He looked over the crowd. "It seems your friend is getting up to leave, along with his friends. Have they paid for their drinks? And left enough that you don't get stiffed?"

Wow, most people didn't worry about the servers or what they got.

"Yes. They gave me the money for what I brought. I didn't let them start a tab." Elliott was definitely smarter than that.

"Good job. Then I'll make sure they leave and don't cause any more trouble. Go on toward the bar and stay there a minute." He flashed what turned out to be a rather nice smile and then made his way toward the table.

Elliott hurried to the bar, watching out for a particular set of eyes and the man who went with them, but he didn't see anything more.

At the bar, he placed his order with Hank and turned to watch the crowd, his heart racing. It was just a sea of guys dancing and doing that all-too-familiar mating ritual in order to entice someone else, one way or another. While Hank made his drinks, Elliott let his mind wander for just a minute. He was so familiar with those movements. Fluidity and grace on the dance floor equaled the same traits in the bedroom, while power and intensity yielded the same. At least that was the theory anyway, the one most of the guys in the club were operating under.

That used to be him. Elliott used to be one of the guys out there on the dance floor. He knew how to shake it like it was hot, because he was hot. Or at least he had been.

"You look far away," Hank said as he set the first of the drinks on the tray.

"Sorry. Just a little more drama than I expected." Elliott sighed and kept his thoughts from sinking back into the past. It didn't matter any longer. What had happened was over. He'd moved away and was trying to build a new life and turn over a new leaf. That was what counted and where he needed to keep his attention.

Hank finished with his order, and Elliott took the tray and headed off. In general, most of the guys had had enough to drink that they were pretty mellow, except for the mean drunks. It was pretty easy to tell who they were, and Elliott steered clear of them.

A large group of guys left his tables a little after midnight and a new group took their places. They seemed intent on nursing their drinks for the rest of the night, which made Elliott's job easier, but it didn't do shit for his tips, which he needed if he was going to make his rent.

"Can I bring you anything?" Elliott asked when he made his next pass.

"No, we're good," one of the guys growled. "They just want us to buy their overpriced drinks." He reached into his pocket and pulled out a bottle, right in front of Elliott, and filled up his buddies' glasses. Elliott left the table to find someone.

"Are you lost?" the huge guy he'd bumped into earlier asked.

"No. I was looking for you. The guys at tables three and four snuck in their own drinks. They have a flask taped to their body or something."

"I'll take care of it," he said. "By the way, what's your name?"

"Elliott."

"Salvatore," he said, and headed over to take care of the problem, which involved some yelling and two other bouncers to pick up a couple of the guys and half carry them out. The others didn't want any trouble and left on their own.

"Thank you," Elliott told Salvatore when he passed him again on his way back to the same tables, which had filled with other groups almost right away.

"No problem…." He looked as though he was about to say something else and stopped himself.

"What?" Elliott asked, a little confused by Salvatore's reaction.

Salvatore shook his head as though he were trying to remove a bad thought or something. "I was about to say 'no problem, cutie,' but that would have been inappropriate." He grinned and turned away.

Elliott stared after the walking wall and actually smiled to himself. At least it was better than being called rabbit or bunny or some such nonsense.

He went back to work, and it wasn't until he was serving the next round of drinks that it hit him. Salvatore thought he was cute.

"LAST CALL" rang through the club, and when the next song ended, the music stopped and the lights came up. Thankfully not too much, but enough to tell the remaining patrons that it was time for them to go home. Elliott settled all his remaining tabs, got everything squared up at the registers, and slipped his tips into his pocket. Then he got to work wiping down the tables and chairs, stacking them up as he went.

"Elliott," Salvatore said as he was finishing up. "There's a guy out front looking for you. He says he's here to take you home."

The blood seemed to drain from his head, and for a second, Elliott thought he might pass out. "What did he look like?" Somehow he managed to get the words out.

"About thirty, with a military haircut, dressed in a suit." Salvatore didn't seem too concerned.

"Was he packing?" Elliott asked, and Salvatore's posture changed completely. "Did he look like he was?"

"Shit…," Salvatore swore under his breath. "I didn't let him in, so I didn't think to check. Why?"

"Ask him for ID because it's after hours. Then say that I'm finishing up and you can't let anyone else inside because it's after last call and it's against the law or something. Make something up." His breathing came in short pants, and Elliott wondered how in the hell he was going to get out of here without being seen. It was probably too late for Salvatore to just say that he had already left. "And once he leaves, get Bull." It was all he could think of, and Elliott found himself hoping that what Bull had said earlier was true, that the people here had his back.

"Why?" Salvatore asked.

Elliott closed his eyes and dropped his rag on the floor. "Because it looks like I'm going to have to leave." And try to get out of here so he could disappear once again. Maybe this time he'd try a bigger city, where he could get lost in the millions of people. He had been stupid to think that he could come to this area and start over. It was too small and there weren't enough places for him to hide. Still, he couldn't figure out how they had found him in the first place, and he needed to know so he didn't make the same mistake again.

CHAPTER 2

"LEAVE? OF course. If you have to go, I can let Bull know. That's not an issue. From the look of things, you're about done, and I can help you out. I mean, if there's a family emergency or something." Salvatore paused to listen to what he'd just said. The guy out front had said that he had come to take Elliott home, and Elliott's first question was if the guy was packing. What the hell kind of family was this kid from? Elliott couldn't have been more than twenty-two or twenty-three at the very most, and while he was cute, the guy was also running scared and jumpy. That was for damned certain.

"Not that kind of leave," Elliott said. "I need to give my notice to Bull and figure out how to get out of here without the guy out front seeing me." He was nervous as hell, shifting his weight from foot to foot, biting his lower lip so hard that it was already red and a little swollen. Salvatore wanted to soothe the abused skin with his finger, but didn't.

"Okay. I'll find Bull, but you need to stay here and don't go anywhere. Promise me." Salvatore made Elliott promise and then hurried to the back. "Bull, I need your help."

"What is it?" Bull asked, looking up from his seat at the desk in the office, where he was preparing the receipts for the night.

"Okay…." Salvatore wasn't sure where to start. "There's guy out front who said he's here to pick up the server Elliott. Said he was going to take him home. I told Elliott, and he went pale, looked like he was going to faint, and then asked me if he was packing. That isn't like any family I know of. Now Elliott is trying to figure out how to give his notice so he can sneak out the back and disappear. This stinks like week-old garbage."

"Sounds like something right up your alley," Harry, Bull's partner in the business, said with a half smile, like this was a normal occurrence.

"Yup. Come on. Let's go have a chat with this guy and see what's up." Bull pushed back the chair and left the office, with Salvatore following right behind. "Elliott," he said as soon as he saw him hovering by the bar.

"I need to go."

Bull shook his head. "You need to stay right here. Who is this man and what does he want with you?"

Elliott blinked like a deer caught in headlights, taking a step back. "It's best if you just let me go and I can get out of here and disappear again. You don't need to get involved in this."

"What?" Bull asked.

"My family. No one deserves to get on their bad side. Just get me out with no one seeing and I'll be out of your hair."

Bull once again shook his head. "That isn't how things work around here." He turned to Salvatore. "Let's go see what we have, shall we?" Bull strode to the front door like he owned the world, unlocked it, and stepped outside. "Can I help you?" he asked with a slight smile.

"I'm here to take Elliott home, and I don't appreciate you keeping me waiting." The man stepped forward, but of course Bull wasn't going to be intimidated.

"He doesn't seem to want to go with you." Bull drew himself up, and Salvatore stood right behind Bull, off to the side. "And it's his choice where he wants to go and with whom. I think it's best if you go and let Elliott decide what he wants to do."

"Look. Elliott's father wants him to come home, so that's what I'm going to do, and I'm willing to go through you to get to him. Why don't you just step aside and send Elliott out so we can take him home and that can be the end of this? No harm, no foul. Otherwise…." He left the threat hanging in the air and unfastened his coat. It was a classic intimidation move.

"I see," Bull said.

Salvatore saw a flash of metal, and before he realized what was happening, Bull had the gun in his hand, ready to wield it like a club.

"Call the police and have them come down here now. Unless this man has a license to carry a concealed weapon here in PA, I say we let the police deal with him." Bull stepped closer. "I'm not someone you or anyone else wants to mess with. I eat little punks like you for breakfast, and you do not get to come near my place and threaten any of the people who work for me. If you do again, you'll feel pain in ways none of you can imagine. And you tell Elliott's father that if he wants his son to come home, that he can use the damned phone and talk to him."

"This isn't going to end well…."

"For you, maybe," Bull told him, and Salvatore was damned impressed. Bull didn't even break a sweat with this guy.

Salvatore got out his phone, called the police, and explained the situation. "They're on their way." He put his phone back in his pocket.

"Good. Now, you sit down, or I'll use this gun as a hammer and thump your skull so damned hard, you won't be able to fucking remember your own mother's name. That is, if you recover at all. And just so you know, it will all be self-defense. I have plenty of witnesses that you can't see and have no idea have been watching you. So, ass on the pavement, now."

The guy didn't move and glared at Bull. Salvatore was ready to act, but Bull swept the guy's feet out from under him with one quick leg movement, sending him sprawling to the concrete sidewalk.

"Jesus."

"He isn't going to help you." Bull pressed his knee to the guy's back. "You decided to do this the hard, painful way." He added additional pressure so his spine stayed right there.

"You're hurting me," the man growled. "You'll pay."

"Actually, I'm fully within my rights. You threatened me with a gun. I disarmed you, and now I'm making sure you can't hurt me or my colleague any further. I could smash your head into the pavement a few times for you." Bull didn't, and they waited as sirens grew closer and then flashing lights pulled up to the curb.

"What do you have, Bull?" the police officer said as he got out of the car.

"Someone that might be interesting to you, Tom. He came here demanding that one of my servers go with him. He threatened me and was carrying concealed. Salvatore can verify my facts for me. You might want to check that he has a permit. He's claiming that he was sent here by the guy's father. What kind of fucking family sends an enforcer to get their son?" Bull set the gun on the pavement a good distance away.

"Did you disarm him?" Officer Tom asked.

"It was a piece of cake," Bull said, and Salvatore figured he was just rubbing it in. "The guy is all intimidation on the outside, with little to back up his mouth."

"We'll take it from here," Officer Tom told him, and took custody of the guy. "You want to give us a name?"

"Go to hell," the guy swore.

Officer Tom simply shrugged. "We'll take him in and find him a really nice cell. Let him think things over with some friends." Tom was clearly enjoying this.

"Thanks." Bull stood, and Officer Tom marched the suspect out to the curb as another car arrived. They got him in the back of the car that arrived, and then Officer Tom approached Bull. "I need to speak to your server and find out what's going on. I suspect this is a pretty hardened guy, and from what you've told me…." He groaned.

"Yeah, I know. I don't like the sound of this at all," Bull said, leading the way inside. Hank and Grant sat with an obviously nervous Elliott. His leg bounced, and he wrung his hands in addition to punishing his lip.

They pulled over chairs, and Salvatore sat next to Elliott keeping an eye on him to try to help keep him calm. "It's okay. We all want to try to help you," he told him gently.

Elliott shook his head and seemed to withdraw further.

"He's right," Officer Tom said. "We have the man in custody on a weapons charge for now. But do you know his name?"

"Roderick Young," Elliott said. "He works for my father. Does the kind of jobs that my father will only trust to him." He sounded small and frightened, his voice quivering a little. "He isn't going to tell you anything, and I suspect that there will be a lawyer at your station within the hour." Elliott sighed. "I thought I had managed to get away from him."

"Your father?" Salvatore asked.

"Yes." The others all turned to him. Elliott seemed to respond to his questions. "Well, my stepfather, anyway." Elliott shivered.

"Why does he want you to come home so badly that he'd send an armed man to get you?"

Elliott sighed and didn't answer. Instead, he looked at each person around him. "I don't want to put all of you in the line of fire, okay? This is a fight between the two of us, and I moved here to get away from him. I didn't tell anyone, and I don't use anything electronic. My phone is one of those you can get at Walmart and have to load minutes on. I do it in cash. I don't have credit cards or even a bank account. Everything is cash."

"But your name? You used your name."

Elliott blushed a little. "I had to use a fake last name. When I decided to try to disappear, I got a new identity. My father isn't the only one who knows people who will do just about anything for a little money. And then I disappeared and came here to try to start over. I needed a chance to have a life of my own." Elliott swallowed. "For all your sakes, just let me go and I'll disappear once again."

"How?" Salvatore asked quietly.

"You think I only got one identity? Why get one when you can get two for the same price?" So Elliott had a sense of humor under all that fear. He turned to Grant. "You all have been nice to me and gave me a chance. I'm sorry I've been as jumpy as a cat and all, but it's best if you all just go on with your lives, let me go, don't ask too many questions, and forget you ever saw or knew me. You can tell Roderick that I did a rabbit, and he'll go back to my stepfather and they can try to find me again." He sighed. "At least all of you will be safe."

Bull stepped forward, stopping Elliott with a glare. "I think it's time you quit your running and told us all what's going on. This isn't helping you or anyone."

"Who is your stepfather?" Officer Tom asked.

Elliott sighed loudly. "Antonio Losquaro."

The name meant nothing to Salvatore, and it didn't seem to register with Bull either. Officer Tom seemed confused. "Should we know him?"

"No. That's the issue. My stepfather controls a lot of things in Pittsburgh, including trucking and garbage collection, stuff like that. He also has his hands in real estate, ladies of the evening, drug distribution, and God knows that else. But no one knows about it. He hides behind a number of associates and entities. Like a modern-day gangster, but with corporate shells and holding companies that make following his path nearly impossible." Elliott stood.

"That doesn't explain why he is so interested in you," Salvatore pointed out.

Elliott paled and clammed up tight.

"Okay," Bull said. "We aren't going to make you say what you don't want to. But know this. Running and hiding isn't the answer, not to something like this. You can go where you want, but if he can find you once, he'll do it again. He obviously has his ways. His associate is in jail, and Tom here is going to do what he can to see that he stays there."

"I better get back to the station so I can build a case fast. If a lawyer is already on the way, I need to have a case for a judge to deny him bail. He's definitely a flight risk."

Elliott snickered. "As soon as you let him loose, he will be out of the state."

Tom smiled. "Good to know." He backed away and pulled Bull aside. They talked softly, and then Officer Tom left the club and Bull returned.

"Hank and Grant, you two go on home and get some rest." They nodded. "And call when you get home so I know you're safe."

"Will do," Hank said, taking Grant's arm, and the two of them left together.

Bull pulled up a chair and sat right in front of Elliott. Salvatore moved closer to Elliott to show a little support.

"I don't want you to go, okay? Running isn't going to help you, and what are you going to do when he finds you again... and again? Because he will and you know it."

"But what about all of you?" Elliott asked.

"I'm not without my skills, and I've dealt with men like your stepfather before. Hell, I've dealt with men much worse than you could ever imagine. It's part of my life from before that seems to keep making an appearance whenever I least expect it. The thing is that you are safer with us than you are alone."

Elliott bowed his head forward. "Why would you all want to help me? I'm just some kid off the street you hired less than a week ago. I'm not worth you all getting hurt over."

Bull placed one of his big hands on Elliott's leg, and it took all Salvatore's self-control not to swipe it away. He hated that Bull was touching him. It didn't matter that it was not in any sexual way or that Bull was devoted to Zach; it sent a wave of irrational jealousy running through him. "Why don't you let us decide what's worth fighting for and what isn't?" Bull nodded. "I've done things that your stepfather can't possibly imagine, so I'm offering you this. If you want to stay, we'll be here with you."

"Why?" Elliott asked, clearly not fathoming what was going on. "No one does something for nothing."

"Maybe where you come from. But here, in this club, and with me, I do things because they're the right thing to do. For years I did things because I was ordered to, and I didn't question it. When it got to be too much, I got the hell out through a miracle. I stopped following orders and followed my heart when I met Zach, and he made me want to do things because they're the right things to do." Bull backed away. "The decision is yours and no one else's."

Elliott didn't move for quite a while, his head hung low. Salvatore hoped he decided to stay, but it seemed as though there was no more fight in him. All that he got from Elliott was the need to run and hide. His entire posture and demeanor screamed scared rabbit. Salvatore hated to see it, but there was nothing he or Bull could do to help someone like that. Bull knew it too, and he stood and put his chair away.

Salvatore sat where he was, determined to wait until Elliott gave them some sort of answer. "What is it to be?" he asked quietly. He could almost see the moment Elliott made his decision.

He took a deep breath and finally raised his gaze. "Okay. I'll stay," he said. "But you don't know what you're getting yourself into."

Bull nodded. "Then tomorrow, before you start work, you and I need to have a talk in my office, and you can tell me exactly what it is you think we're in for. No one can fight without information, and you're going to have to tell us everything you can about your stepfather and his operations."

"Okay." Elliott seemed resigned to it.

"For tonight, you need a safe place that you can stay. Don't think about going near your apartment. If your stepfather is as you say, that will be watched already."

"He can stay with me. I have the room at my place, and it isn't like anyone is going to connect me with him," Salvatore offered. "I live just up north in Italian Lake, and at this time of night, no one is around, so anyone following is going to stick out like a sore thumb."

Spook came in through the back to join them. He was one of Bull's colleagues and also worked security at the club. "There are no tracking devices on any of the cars, and as near as I can tell, our visitor came alone." Sometimes it was creepy just how much Spook knew, and yet he was rarely seen—hence the name. The man had superpowers. "I'll make sure they get out of here with no one seeing, and then I'm going to go home." He patted Bull on the shoulder and quietly left the room.

"Take him home and watch out for him," Bull said gently. "I'll see you tomorrow."

Elliott shook his head. "You don't even know what my stepfather is capable of."

Bull stopped and turned around. "Elliott, your stepfather has no idea what *I'm* capable of, and I think he's the one who should be worried." He turned away and left the floor.

"Come on. Let's get out of here. I don't know about you, but I could use something to eat and then a soft bed for a few hours." Salvatore did his best to stifle the threatening yawn, but failed. It was nearly three in the morning, and the summer sun would be rising soon enough.

"Yeah, I'm hungry too," Elliott said, getting to his feet.

Salvatore took care of the chairs, and then he and Elliott left the club by the back door. "Where's your car?"

"I walked," Elliott explained. Salvatore figured it was one additional way that Elliott could stay off the grid. If he didn't have a car, he didn't have to register it with the state.

"That one's mine." Salvatore pointed. He was pretty proud of his dark red Mustang convertible. He had gotten it used just a year ago. The previous owner had worked from home, so they didn't drive it very much and it was in pristine condition. He unlocked the doors, and Elliott slid into the passenger seat. For a second, Salvatore watched Elliott, a little envious of the leather as it cradled Elliott. He got in and pressed the starter button, and the car roared to life. Normally on a warm night like this, he would put the top down and let the wind blow through his hair. But tonight he left it up and turned on the air-conditioning, pulled out of the staff parking area, and headed north down Third Street toward home.

"Why are you doing this?" Elliott asked. "You have to want something."

Salvatore gripped the wheel a little tighter. "Not everyone is like your stepfather or the people he associates with. Most people are like me and Bull, who will help others because it's the right thing to do."

"How long have you known Bull?"

"Oh, maybe eight years or so. He and I were in a unit together some time ago. Bull got out, and I stayed in for a while after that. Then I wanted out too." Salvatore knew he was being cryptic, but it wasn't like he could just explain all the things he'd been involved in, so it was better to be vague. "I asked Bull for a job, and he hired me because some of his security guys hadn't been doing their jobs, and I can see now that he was right."

"Will the guys get fired for letting that booze in?"

"That I don't know, but Bull knows who it was and he'll be talking to them. Meanwhile, starting tomorrow, I'll be out on the front doors, and I intend to watch out for guys like that and anyone you tell me I should look for." Salvatore pulled up to a light and checked the rearview mirror. There was no one behind him, and he hadn't seen another car. Once the light changed, he continued through and made the turn onto his wide, quiet residential street.

The ranch home had been built in the sixties, and Salvatore had so many plans for it. The house had a great layout, but was incredibly dated. At least he'd had a chance to work on the outside. He pulled into the garage and closed the overhead door, then locked it while Elliott got out of the car.

He opened the house, and they went inside, where he turned on the lights. Elliott looked a little shell-shocked, not that Salvatore could blame him. "This isn't my idea of decorating. I bought the house and haven't had a chance to change much."

"But the seashell wallpaper is so you," Elliott quipped.

"Yeah, I know. I was thinking of doing the entire house around it." Salvatore broke into laughter, and Elliott relaxed. He had been wound tightly for a while, and it was good to see him let loose a little. "I'm planning to clear this entire section of the house and open it all up into a huge great room with a dining area, kitchen, and plenty of living space. But that's going to take some time." He set his things on the counter and opened the refrigerator. "I have some pasta I can reheat."

"That would be nice," Elliott said, sitting at the table.

Salvatore got out two bowls, portioned out the food, and stuck the first bowl in the microwave. "Do you want a beer?" he asked, turning to Elliott, who seemed to be doing his best to make himself seem as small and inconspicuous as possible. Shit, what in the hell had this family of his done to him? Salvatore got out two Coronas and put them on the table, along with some leftover salad from the refrigerator. It was probably a carb overload, but after a long day, he was hungry. When the microwave dinged, he put the bowl in front of

Elliott and got him utensils. "No one is going to yell at you or come at you. Just relax." He lightly touched Elliot's shoulder.

Elliott nodded, and some of the tension left his shoulders, but not all of it by far. Still, he ate slowly as Salvatore heated up his bowl. "This is really good."

"My mom taught me how to make the sauce. She makes some of the best and gave me her secrets." He leaned against the counter, opening the beer and taking a swig. God, that felt good going down. It had been too long since he'd had something cold.

"Does she live here?" Elliott asked just above a whisper.

"Philadelphia. That's where I was raised, and she lives in the same house I grew up in. I thought of settling there, but I needed to make a life of my own." He got his bowl from the microwave. "My dad died when I was a kid, and Mom raised me alone. When I was a teenager, she lost her job. She started working in restaurants to make ends meet and discovered her real passion. Now she has a small restaurant that has a waiting list three months long." Salvatore was so proud of her. "After I got out of the Navy and then finished the private operational work, she wanted me to go work for her. Food is her passion, not mine."

"It doesn't taste like it," Elliott said between bites.

"Thank you. But it's true. I can cook, but it isn't my passion." Salvatore finished off his pasta and took the bowl to the sink to rinse out. "I like doing security work. It's the kind of thing I was trained for." He still felt like a dope for not thinking to check if the guy coming for Elliott had a gun. But the idea had never occurred to him. He seemed like a relative or someone who was giving him a ride. "How about you? What's your passion?"

"I don't know. Pokémon cards when I was a kid. My mom used to buy them for me when she went to the store. There was a place that sold them in the same plaza, and she would bring some home for me." Elliott smiled when he talked about his mom.

"Do you not get along with her now?" This whole thing with Elliott's family had disturbed Salvatore to the core. His mom was his rock, a close friend, and someone he couldn't imagine wanting to run away from.

"I get along with my mom just fine." Elliott finished and pushed the bowl away, then drank from his bottle. "She doesn't know about my stepfather. She thinks he's this successful businessman who loves her and takes good care of her and her son." He shook his head. "She doesn't know what he does and how he acts toward people who disagree with him."

Salvatore sat back down, putting his beer on the table with a *thunk*. "Why is he so keen to get you to come home?"

Elliott turned away. "I can't tell you. Standing up for me is one thing, and I'm not sure you should be doing that. But if I share stuff with you, it will make the target on your back even bigger."

Salvatore nodded. "You saw something or heard something you shouldn't have, and now he wants you where he can control you." It seemed pretty simple to him. Hell, it was the plot of a million movies.

"No. That isn't it. I…." Elliott leaned over the table. "I have a number of papers and records. I found out that he's a crook, and I made sure that I had proof. I copied some records and ledgers, as well as tax information. Then I hid it as insurance before I left. He doesn't know about all that stuff, but he's scared to death that I might know something."

"So he wants to shut you up?" Salvatore asked, half to himself. He didn't really need an answer. He wasn't going to press for anything else right now. He was tired, and Elliott looked like he was going to keel over on the table at any minute. There was a good chance he might have a pretty good idea of what was happening, at least at a high level. That was plenty for now. "Why don't I show you where the guest room is? You can clean up and try to get some rest."

Salvatore took care of the rest of the dishes and then the empty beer bottles before leading Elliott down the hall to his guest room. It was modest, with just a bed and a dresser, but it would work, and the sheets were clean. "I'll put out some towels and things in the bathroom across the hall. I think I have some travel-size stuff in there, and an extra toothbrush. I'll put those out as well."

"Thank you," Elliott said, standing in the doorway of the guest room, appearing kind of lost. His eyes had a basset hound expression, and Salvatore wanted to somehow make it better.

"It will be okay. The house is locked up, and there's no way anyone can know where you are right now. Do you have a phone?" he asked as a precaution.

"Yes. A burner, like I told you." Elliott showed it to him, and Salvatore turned it over and quickly removed the battery.

"Phones ping towers, and if anyone is looking for you, they can get a general area. Granted, they would need to know the number to get to you and that isn't likely, but better safe than sorry. Now at least that avenue is closed to them." He flashed a half smile. "Any idea how they found you?"

Elliott shrugged. "The only way I can think of is because I called my mom on the house phone and she answered. I didn't call her cell because I knew it could be traced, and I even blocked the number just in case. That was the only thing I did, because I didn't want her to worry."

"Do you think she told your stepfather?"

"Yeah. I knew she would. I didn't tell her where I was, just that I needed to be on my own for a while and that I was safe and would contact her again soon. She tells my stepfather everything because she trusts the old bastard."

"It's okay. We can talk it over with Bull and Spook in the morning. Just try to get some rest. We'll all be able to think more clearly after we have some sleep." He left Elliott alone in the guest room while he got towels and stuff out in the bathroom for Elliott. After leaving the things he might need on the counter, Salvatore went to his own room and closed the door.

He went to his small en suite bath and turned on the water. He needed to get the smell of work and sweat off himself. When the water was hot, he slipped under the spray and washed himself quickly. His mind kept going to the fact that Elliott was in his house. A tingle of excitement ran through him, but there was no time to do anything about it. Salvatore needed to shower quickly so there would be hot water left for Elliott. So he washed fast and turned off the water, dried himself, and then wound the towel around his waist.

The house seemed very still as he returned to his bedroom. Salvatore cracked his door open to see if he heard Elliott moving around, but all he heard was the soft hum when the refrigerator kicked on. It was too quiet. He left the room to check the other bath, just as Elliott's door opened and he stepped into the hall.

Elliott nearly ran into him, and Salvatore felt his gaze travel up him slowly. Damn, the heat in those eyes was stunning. Finally, Elliott turned away and raced to the bathroom, closing the door.

"Is there anything else you need?"

"No" came the broken reply.

"Okay. I'll see you in the morning." Salvatore rechecked that the house was locked up and turned out the lights. He went back to his room and shut the door once again. Salvatore hadn't intended to make him uncomfortable or to supply some kind of free show.

Salvatore hung up his towel in the bathroom and climbed into bed. But like so many times before when he was keyed up or excited, he couldn't fall to sleep. His mind jumped from Elliott in the guest room to missions he had been on where he'd had to stay awake. Usually he could kick his military training into gear and sleep almost on command, but not tonight. He had someone in his house who was counting on him to help keep him safe, and Salvatore wasn't going to let him down. Not that he really thought of Elliott like one of his missions, but maybe this was like that to a degree. And he'd had more than his share of losses on the battlefield, said goodbye to more than his share of friends, though even one was way too many. Still, he didn't intend to be adding to that total any time soon.

Every creak sent his senses into overdrive, and more than once he thought he might have heard Elliott in the other room. He couldn't have been sleeping very well either. After an additional hour, the sounds dissipated and the house grew quieter. Salvatore hoped that Elliott was asleep and resting. They had a big day tomorrow, and Elliott was going to need it.

Salvatore, on the other hand, couldn't seem to calm his mind, and it took hours before he was able to stop worrying and wondering about Elliott and what was going on.

CHAPTER 3

ELLIOTT WASN'T sure what time it was when he woke, but light shone through the windows. He sat up and rubbed his eyes as everything came back to him. His stepfather had found him, and he was staying at Salvatore's house. He shook his head and tried to figure some shit out. He had only met Salvatore last night, and here he was in his guest room, putting his trust in the guy to try to keep him safe. Not that anyone was going to be able to do that if his stepfather decided to bring his power to bear on the situation.

He should have just gone and not said anything to anyone. Now he had pulled these other people into his family mess.

"Elliott," Salvatore said from outside the door.

"Yes?" Elliott said, pulling himself out of his thoughts.

"I made some breakfast."

Of course he had. Salvatore was a nice man. And from what Elliott had seen last night with him just wearing a towel, a mighty fine, hunky nice man at that.

"Thank you." He got out of the bed and pulled on the same clothes he'd been wearing the night before. Somehow, he really needed to go back to the apartment and get some things to wear, but he didn't know if that was a good idea. Elliott doubted his stepfather had actually sent a whole bunch of people into town, so if Roderick was still in jail, it was probably safe for him to return. If he wasn't, then his stepfather already knew what was going on and was formulating his next move.

Elliott left the bedroom and found the table set with plates and glasses of juice. The room smelled of bacon and eggs, and when the toaster popped, Salvatore put a half bagel on each plate.

"Go ahead and sit down before it gets cold. I have butter and cream cheese for the bagels, and I'll bring the rest over."

"Do you usually eat like this?" Elliott asked as he sat, wondering how he was going to eat the mountain of food.

"Most of the time, yeah." Salvatore added eggs and bacon to the plate and then filled his own before putting the pans back on the stove and sitting down. "It's breakfast, and we were up until three, active and running around. It's almost noon and I'm hungry. Aren't you? Where do you get all that energy from if you don't eat?"

Elliott spread butter and cream cheese on his bagel. They were his weakness when it came to breakfast. He could eat them every day, and Salvatore had the good kind with the onion-and-garlic cream cheese. *Yummy.* "When is Bull expecting us?"

"A message came through an hour ago. He said he'd meet us at the club at five. Bull also said that someone would stop by the house in a few hours with a bag for you. He didn't want you going to your place, so he sent someone."

"To my apartment?" Elliott hated that idea. That apartment, while dinky small, was the first home of his own he'd ever had, and the thought of someone going in there, even though it was to help him, made his nerves spike again.

"It was probably Spook, and he just got you some clothes and things. It really isn't anything to worry about. I swear that guy sees everything everyone does in that club. He knows what he needs to see and what he needs to forget." Salvatore continued eating. "Go ahead and finish up."

"But…."

"It isn't safe for you to go—you have to know that. I can tell you're upset, but you're safe here. Bull also said that Roderick is still in jail. Lawyers did show up, but the police convinced a judge that he's a flight risk, so bail was denied. And he didn't have a license to carry concealed. Weapons charges aren't taken lightly, especially in light of the threats that he made to a prominent business owner in the community." Salvatore seemed pretty pleased.

"It's likely my stepfather will just send someone else."

"True. But now he has to go to extra effort, and in addition he has to figure out what he's going to do with Roderick. Your stepfather is getting further and further in. He has to be deciding if he should just leave well enough alone and cut his losses."

Elliott shook his head. "He'll never do that. He has to get me back where he can control me. Otherwise he doesn't know what I have on him or how I might use it. Granted, he still has one big bargaining chip: my mother. He's never hurt her, and in his own way, I think he loves her, but who knows how far he'll go?" Elliott ate the last of his bagel and a few bites of the eggs before munching on bacon. "It's hard to tell with him."

"Has he threatened her, as far as you know?"

"No. And she adores him and is totally blind to anything he does. He's also really careful to make sure she is completely unaware of most of his activities. This isn't like in the movies where the wives know and close their eyes to things. He keeps it from her."

"Well, finish eating and try not to worry. You aren't alone now. There are people who have your back."

Elliott shrugged. "I still don't understand why you care so much. No one else has. I even tried to tell my mother, but she thought I was crazy and had to have made a mistake." That had been the day he knew he had to get out or he was going to end up spending the rest of his life under his stepfather's thumb.

"I don't think I can explain it better than I already have. You just need to trust us, I guess." Salvatore finished eating and took care of the dishes. "You need to tell Bull everything you know. We can't prepare for everything, but the more we know, the better the plans to build our defenses will be."

"Or the more you know, the bigger danger you're going to put yourself in," Elliott retorted.

"Maybe." Salvatore leaned over the table. "You have a choice, and no one else can make it for you. Me, Bull, and the other guys at the club are willing to stand behind you. We've only known you a few days, but we have your back, because that's what family does. I don't know about the people you come from, and based on what you've told me, it's pretty fucked up."

"To say the least." Elliott wished he could argue about that.

27

"You can run if you want. None of us will stop you. After all, you're an adult, and trying to keep you here would make us no better than your stepfather." Salvatore's understanding gaze told him that he was better than that. "I learned in the Navy that there are times when we all have to decide who we are."

"When was yours?" Elliott asked. Salvatore fascinated him. Here was a guy willing to put himself on the line for a near stranger. That made him curious about the kind of man he was. Not that Elliott was buying the whole "we don't want anything from you" thing just yet. But he was becoming more willing to see what Salvatore and the guys at the club were about.

"The first time my ship was under attack. I realized I could shit my pants and run for as much cover as I could get, or do my job and shoot the bastard planes out of the sky. I sat still and shot down two of the motherfuckers. Running has its place, but if I had run at that time, under fire, I would never have earned the respect of the men around me and I'd have eventually washed out of the Navy. It's that simple. A coward dies a million deaths—a hero just one. Because each time you run and don't stand up for yourself, a little piece of who you are dies."

Elliott glanced up at the ceiling. He wasn't so sure that was true. "Or a hero dies young and stupid."

Salvatore glared at him. "You can run if you want, but you'll be running forever. Your stepfather will find you, again and again. Either that, or you'll be looking over your shoulder for the rest of your life, wondering if he's right behind you. Is that the kind of life you want?"

"No, of course not. But I don't see how you, Bull, and Spook, as well as the rest of you, are going to put a stop to him. My stepfather can be ruthless as shit."

"Maybe. But you told me you had to get out. That you couldn't stay at home after your mother didn't believe you. It took guts and strength to leave." Salvatore drew even closer. "Find that same strength to fight for what you have." He straightened up and pushed the chair back without another word, left the table, and strode down the hall.

Elliott watched him go, unable to ignore the determination in his steps… or the way his muscles rolled and flexed under his jeans with each stride. There was power there, and Elliott wished he had some of that strength to draw on. Instead, he felt empty and tired, like he was all used up and should just say to hell with it.

"Fighting for what you want and to have your own life is worth whatever you have to do," Salvatore said, stopping and turning back to him.

"That's easy for you to say. You look like that and can beat the shit out of just about anyone. What in the hell do I have to fight with?" Elliott asked, and Salvatore came back to where Elliott was and cupped Elliott's cheeks in his hands.

"You have this—your brain. That's the most important fighting weapon. Punching and hitting is one thing, but being smart—knowing your opponent, finding out where he's weakest and then hitting him there—takes brains and thinking, not fists, and I think you have plenty of that."

The heat from his hands warmed Elliott's skin, and he closed his eyes. Part of him just wanted to concentrate on that strong yet gentle touch, to soak in that heat and the intimacy, even if it was an illusion of something more. His head kept warring with his body. Elliott knew that what Salvatore said was right and that he should stay and fight, but his body was ready to jump up and run.

"I can feel the battle inside you," Salvatore said softly. "I know what you're feeling because I've been there."

"Yeah, but you're a hero," Elliott countered.

"Everyone is a hero. It isn't just guys like me. We all have the power inside us to be a hero or to run. We get a choice. That doesn't mean that everything always turns out. I lost friends in combat, and I did everything I should have done. Once I carried one of them over my shoulder so I could get him to the medic, but he didn't make it. I wasn't fast enough. At least that's what I thought at the time. But

I couldn't have done more, and he still died." Salvatore's eyes grew dark and filled with pain.

"Was he more than a friend?" Elliott asked, getting a clear picture in his mind of the hurt in Salvatore's eyes.

Salvatore nodded. "He could have been my world, but he and I never got enough time to find out. And then he was gone. I know now that I did all I could, and if I had it to do over, I'd probably do the same thing again and all I could do is hope for a different result."

"Okay," Elliott said softly. "I'll stay. I just don't want anyone else to get hurt on my account."

Salvatore smiled, and Elliott thought he might lean closer. He didn't dare move and began to close his eyes, thinking that maybe Salvatore was going to kiss him. Instead, the warm hands slipped away. "Oh," Salvatore breathed. "I see what you were expecting."

Elliott blinked. "I wasn't expecting anything." He cleared his throat and tried to think of something to cover his thoughts. "When did you say this person was going to bring my things?" He went into the extremely dated living room and peered out the window, Salvatore following him. "I guess it would be nice to have some clean clothes." He took a deep breath and willed his pulse to slow a little. He'd been so stupid to think that Salvatore might be interested in him that way. "I have to work tonight, and I don't want to have to go in wearing the same clothes I did last night."

"He'll be here soon enough," Salvatore said. "I usually try to do my shopping and things for the week in one trip, but I don't think it's a good idea for you to be out and about."

"As long as Roderick is locked up, I should be fine."

"Where does your stepfather live?" Salvatore asked.

"Right now, Pittsburgh. He and my mother live in one of those mansions in the hills. They have a private path up to their place from the street below. In the movies, gangsters and criminals usually keep a low profile. Not my stepfather. He has a huge social calendar and knows everyone who's anyone. If something happens that he doesn't like, my stepfather can press his influence to bring it all to an end. It's what he's really good at."

"I see."

Elliott let the curtain fall back into place. "No, you don't. A few years ago, a new district attorney was elected, and he was going to clean up the city and get rid of the kind of people who skirted the law. When he went after my stepfather, suddenly that district attorney came under fire for some alleged activity. I have little doubt that it was cooked up and then spread by my stepfather's people. In the end, he got drummed out of office and a replacement was appointed. The entire affair died after that, and my stepfather went on as though nothing had happened. He has police and other useful people within his social circle."

"I see. So it isn't going to take him all that long to find someone else to come and take Roderick's place?"

Elliott shrugged. "I don't know. Roderick is his right-hand man. If there's dirty shit, Roderick knows where the bodies are buried. If I could, I'd tell the police to lean on him hard, do whatever they can to get him to talk, because he knows a hell of a lot." He grew quiet. Maybe it was a good idea that he was going to meet with Bull and the guys. If they knew what to do, then maybe he wouldn't have to be the one to face all this alone.

"Are you feeling better?"

"I think so. If nothing more, then I can tell someone else what I saw and heard, and maybe they'll believe me." It had hurt like a knife that his mother had dismissed what he'd tried to tell her out of hand. "At least I'll talk about what I know."

"That's the spirit."

When the bell rang, Salvatore answered the door, and Spook stepped inside with a suitcase. It was one from Elliott's set of luggage, something his mom had bought for him when he'd taken a school trip with the French Club the summer before senior year. Elliott had to admit that his stepfather's ill-gotten gains had gone a long way toward making his life easier and better. There were vacations, and he'd had the chance to do things that most kids didn't. And he'd taken advantage of all of it until he'd found out exactly how his stepfather got his money. Suddenly all that travel and the gifts from his stepfather and mother were tainted. Even the suitcase seemed like it belonged to someone else.

"Thank you."

"You're welcome. It didn't seem like anyone had been there. But I set it up so we'll know if someone tries to get in. I just packed a few things for you. If you need something else, let me know, and I can get it for you."

Elliott wasn't so sure how he felt about doing that, but Spook at least seemed to be discreet and didn't talk about anything he might have seen while in the apartment. Not that Elliott had kinky stuff or anything, but his home, even as small as it was, held his personal things. "I appreciate it."

"Are you hungry?" Salvatore asked Spook. "Or do you need something to drink?"

"No. I have to get home. I promised that I'd take Jeremy out to the go-kart track. He loves it, and we always have so much fun. I'll see you at work later," he said, then left.

Elliott took the suitcase down to the room he was using. Spook had brought his shaving kit, as well as an assortment of clothes and things. Elliott stripped off the clothes he'd been wearing and pulled on fresh. His skin instantly felt better, and he sighed, folding the dirty clothes and setting them aside.

He wasn't sure what he was going to do for the next few hours until he was supposed to go in and talk with Bull at the club. The television flipped on in the living room, and the roar of a crowd entered the bedroom through the closed door. Salvatore was watching sports of some kind. Not that Elliott was interested, particularly, but he went and sat with him.

"Come on, that was a strike. Are you blind?" Salvatore yelled at the television, leaning forward in his chair.

Elliott had watched baseball sometimes. His stepfather had taken him to Pittsburgh Pirates games on occasion. Mostly when he was having some sort of shindig at a game, and then they ended up in one of the enclosed, air-conditioned boxes. Everyone drank, talked, and halfheartedly watched the game between bites of caviar on toast.

He knew now it was his stepfather's way of networking and getting various people in public life indebted to him so that later he could ask favors they didn't dare refuse.

"Do you always yell at the television?" Elliott teased. "Are you one of those people who thinks he knows better than everyone else what calls the umpire should make?"

"I don't think it—I know, and that ump is as blind as a bat. Even I could see from here that was a... oh-ho...." He jumped to his feet as the bat cracked and the ball sailed high. "Home run!" Salvatore grinned as he sat down, rubbing his hand. "That's going to be hard to come back from."

Elliott sat watching the rest of the game, which seemed anticlimactic. The fight appeared to have left the other team, and the game came to an easy close. He wondered what Salvatore would watch next, but he flipped the channel to another game and settled in to watch.

"I take it you like baseball," Elliott said.

"I love football, but the season hasn't started yet, so I watch baseball." To Elliott's surprise, Salvatore handed over the remote. "If there's something else you'd rather watch, go ahead."

"You sure?" Elliott asked, then clicked through the stations once Salvatore nodded. There wasn't much interesting until he found the Errol Flynn *Adventures of Robin Hood*. It was old and had grown campy with age, but Elliott glanced at Salvatore, who didn't seem to mind, so he kept it on. "I love Olivia de Havilland. I think she was just gorgeous, and this is before she did *Gone with the Wind*." He settled back.

"It's fun."

Elliott turned so he could see Salvatore. "Are you sure it's okay? I could go in the other room and find something to read so you can watch baseball."

"No. This is a fun movie, I haven't seen it in a long time, and we should watch something we both like." Salvatore got up, and Elliott heard the jingle of bottles in the refrigerator. "Do you want a soda or something? I have beer too, but it's a little early considering we only had breakfast not too long ago."

"A Coke is great. Thank you," Elliott said, and Salvatore handed him one when he came back in, the two of them settling in to watch the old movie. "I wanted to be Robin Hood when I was a kid. To be able to swing through the trees and shoot arrows at the bad guys."

"I wanted to be a cop. When I joined the service, I thought about trying to be an MP, but they had so many other things that interested me by then, I went in a different way. I found out I could think quickly on my feet, was strong, and had incredible endurance. So I went with my strengths."

"That's pretty obvious," Elliott quipped, and Salvatore grinned and flexed his arm. "Now you're just showing off." He chuckled as Salvatore struck a pose. "Or was that what you were doing last night?" He was afraid he might have gone too far by bringing up the towel incident, but Salvatore joined his laughter.

"That was purely accidental."

"Okay. Well, it was quite a view before going to bed, I can tell you that." Elliott wanted to slap his hand over his mouth. Sometimes he needed to remember that it wasn't necessary to say the first thing that came into his head. "Sorry."

Salvatore got to his feet. "I'm not embarrassed. I worked really hard to build my body. In the service, I needed the strength and raw power. When I did black ops, I needed it to be able to extract people from difficult situations. And it might seem weird, but we also get strong so that if we get injured, we can hopefully come back faster."

"But you're more than just muscle." Elliott wished he hadn't said something so ridiculously stereotypical.

"I'd like to think so. I like working out. It gives me a way to work off my excess aggression, and when things get stressful, I hit the gym and pound as much iron as I can." Salvatore struck a pose that had his muscles bulging, and Elliot wondered if his shirt was going to rip at the sleeves. After a few seconds, Salvatore relaxed and grinned. "Sorry."

Elliott swallowed hard. "Don't be, not on my account." That had been one hell of a view. "Just don't do the dancing pecs thing."

"Oh God, no. That's just kind of tacky."

Salvatore sat back down, and they continued watching the movie. Elliott couldn't help wondering if Salvatore had been playing with him or if he was actually flirting. Of course, he wasn't going to be able to ask because he didn't want to feel like a fool.

"Have you ever worked out?"

Elliott looked down at himself and laughed nervously. "No. I'm not exactly the kind of guy who is going to feel at home in a place like that."

"We could go if you want. I have a membership, and I can bring a guest." Salvatore leaned forward. "I know you feel like things are a little out of control sometimes. You don't need to get bulky or anything if you don't want to, but working out gets you in tune with your body and muscles. You might like it." He sat back again, and Elliott found himself agreeing before he could really think too much about it. "Awesome." Salvatore jumped to his feet.

"Did you mean right now?" Elliott hadn't considered the idea that he meant immediately.

"Why not? The movie will still be here when we want to watch it. I usually go to the gym in the afternoon. It's quiet about this time since most people go in the morning or after work. Do you have clothes and things you can wear?"

Elliott doubted it. "I have some T-shirts and stuff. There might be a pair of shorts in my apartment, but I doubt there's anything in what Spook brought."

"No problem." Salvatore left the room, and Elliott wondered what he had gotten himself into. He had no clue about gyms and weights, and the place was going to be filled with guys who could snap him in half. Salvatore returned just as Elliott's imagination went into total overdrive. He handed Elliott a small red duffel. "I found some shorts that are too small for me, so they should work. I also put a towel in there for you."

35

Jesus, if he went to the gym, he was going to have to change and shower there. Now that was scary. He hadn't done that since high school, and it had given him the heebie-jeebies then.

"Go get a T-shirt and some fresh underwear, and we'll go." Salvatore seemed so damned excited that Elliott did as he asked and met him by the garage door, where Salvatore was hanging up the phone. "Roderick's attorney is apparently causing trouble, but he isn't going anywhere according to Bull." He opened the door and stepped into the garage, took Elliott's bag, and put it in the saddlebag of a huge motorcycle.

"You want to take that?" Elliott asked.

"We can take the car, but it's a great day. I have another helmet, and frankly, it's maneuverable and fast as all hell."

Elliott smiled. He had always wanted to ride a motorcycle, but his mother would have nothing of it and forbade him to ever get on one. "Let's go."

"Cool." Salvatore handed him the helmet, and Elliott put it on while Salvatore wheeled the bike out of the garage and closed the door. Salvatore got on, and Elliott straddled the bike behind him, the seat surprisingly comfortable. "Hold on to me," he instructed, starting the engine.

Elliott encircled Salvatore's waist with his hands and held on tightly as they started forward. "This is great," he said as they glided down the road, heading toward downtown briefly before turning east and picking up speed. The capitol area fell off behind them as they continued moving, the bike vibrating beneath him. Elliott held a little tighter and tried not to notice Salvatore's hard belly or the way his scent seemed to pull him in regardless of how fast they went.

Exhilarating. That was the only way he could describe the ride. The open air, the rush of the wind, the vibration of the engine—all of it worked its magic on him, and soon enough he realized he was hard as a rock with his cock pressed right against Salvatore's ass, and damn, did it feel good. He backed away a little so Salvatore didn't think he was being too forward.

At a stoplight, Salvatore put his feet down to keep the bike upright, and when the light changed, he took off. Elliott tightened his grip and found himself once again plastered to Salvatore's back. Not that he was complaining, and if Salvatore didn't like it, then it was his own fault.

After riding for about fifteen minutes, they turned into a large shopping center and drove up to the door of the gym. Salvatore parked, and Elliott got off the bike and pulled the helmet off. They got their bags and went inside, where Salvatore signed them in while Elliott looked the place over. It was clean and there were quite a few women there, which made him feel better because he would be less on display.

"Are you ready?"

"I guess." Elliott had no idea what he was going to do and followed Salvatore through the club and back to the locker rooms.

"You can take any one you like."

Elliott opened the nearest one that wasn't locked and started taking off his shoes. He was determined not to look around and concentrated on changing his clothes.

"Sal," a deep voice said.

Elliott turned in time to see a guy in nothing but a jockstrap standing next to Salvatore. He was huge, with an ass that could crack walnuts. Elliott looked away and swallowed hard as he finished getting dressed. Salvatore and the guy talked a few minutes, and by the time they were done, Elliott was dressed and sat down on a bench to pull on his shoes.

He checked to see if Salvatore was ready to go and got one hell of a view, even more than he'd had with the towel. Elliott's mouth watered at the sight of Salvatore's tight, hard backside. He knew he should look away, but he couldn't help it, and when Salvatore turned around, Elliott found himself at eye level with his big, thick cock. Now he had to lower his gaze.

"Umm, I'll meet you out there," he stammered, hurrying out of the area, breathing deeply as he leaned against the wall outside the locker room. Jesus, he hadn't come here to perv on anyone, but it seemed that almost everywhere he looked, eye candy abounded.

Eventually Salvatore joined him, wearing blue shorts and a tank top that hugged every muscle of his chest. How in the hell was Elliott going to make it through any kind of workout session without popping wood and embarrassing himself all to hell?

"Come on. We need to warm up before we start anything. We can start with some stretches and then do a few minutes of cardio. The stretches get your muscles limber, and the cardio gets your heart pumping. You should do both before you start lifting, especially since this is your first time."

Elliott followed Salvatore to a section of the floor covered with mats, and they sat down. Salvatore showed him how to stretch his thighs and calves, then his chest by holding something solid—in this case, Salvatore's arm—and slowly twisting to elongate the muscle. The thing was, Elliott had no trouble at all concentrating on the hard muscle under his hand, which only made his ongoing problem all the more urgent.

"I think we can start. Why don't we try a stationary bike for six minutes and then we'll go from there?"

Elliott could ride a bike. "All right." He took the one next to Salvatore and started pedaling, which started the machine, and Salvatore helped him set it up. "This is pretty easy."

"It's supposed to be. We want to get our muscles moving and our heart beating a little faster. Gets the blood to all the places we want it. After this, we'll lift a little." Salvatore flashed a smile and went back to pumping his legs, which Elliott found fascinating, especially the way his legs stretched the material of his shorts. Hell, Elliott needed to admit that Salvatore was as hot a guy as he had ever seen. With that little epiphany, he turned away, because a guy like Salvatore was not going to be interested in a skinny little guy like him.

"Hey, Sal," a man said as he approached. They fist-bumped as Salvatore kept moving. "What have you been up to?"

"Got a new job."

The guy turned to Elliott. "You training other guys now or something?"

Salvatore shook his head. "Elliott, this is Ivan. He's in training for a bodybuilding competition in California in a few weeks. Elliott and I are just working out together. He's a friend."

Ivan fist-bumped him too. "Cool. This your first time?"

"Does it show?" Elliott asked. "Yeah. Salvatore brought me along with him."

"This is a good gym. The equipment is in good shape, and there are plenty of weights and stuff." For a second Elliott thought Ivan might be checking him out. "Are you two... together?" Ivan asked, and Salvatore shook his head.

"Elliott is a guy from work. Be nice to him." The last part came out like a soft growl.

"I didn't mean anything." Ivan patted the display in front of him. "You're all kinds of cute and all." He smiled as Elliott blushed big-time.

"Oh, for goodness sake. Go lift something and stop hitting on Elliott. I know you think you're God's gift to... well, everyone... but geez. Take your hotness and go charm Dennis over there. He's been watching you the entire time you've been over here." There was no heat in Salvatore's admonition, but the look in his eyes told a different story.

"Okay." Ivan took a few steps and then turned back. "But I still think you're cute." Then he walked away, and Elliott found himself looking down at his feet to hide his smile. Not that one of his aspirations was to be thought of as cute, but he wasn't going to turn it down.

"Ivan flirts with everyone. Don't give it too much thought," Salvatore told him.

"Oh...." Elliott pumped harder and figured it was best not to think too much about it. "So he says stuff like that to everyone."

"You mean the cute thing? No. That's a new one," Salvatore told him. "Though I have to agree with him. You are cute." It was accompanied by a wink, and Elliott wondered if Salvatore was flirting now. Elliott liked that Salvatore thought he was cute.

39

"And you're so smoking hot, I might get burned." Elliott had meant to be clever, but the words came out more seriously than he intended. "I mean…." Now he was blushing even more, and he turned away from Salvatore, concentrating on the lights on the display and wishing the floor would open up and swallow him whole. Not that he hadn't been truthful. Salvatore was as hot and sexy as any guy he had ever met, but to actually say something…. He felt like a fool. Yeah, he'd said he thought Elliott was cute, but so were bunnies and puppies. That didn't mean he wanted to fuck them. In fact, that was really gross, and…. God, maybe he needed to go back into the locker room and just hide in one of the bathroom stalls until Salvatore was ready to leave. That was sounding like a better and better idea by the second.

Salvatore ended his workout, sitting still on the bike. "You can stop pedaling and the machine will turn off."

"Okay." Maybe Salvatore was going to just pretend he hadn't said something stupid. "Where to next?"

"Since this is your first time, we're going to do a whole-body workout. I usually concentrate on one or two muscles a day, but starting out, you don't want to overdo it." He led the way toward one of the flat bench-press things at the back of the gym and began stripping off the weights. "We can take it light. Just get used to the movement and the weight. I'll spot you so you don't have to worry about anything."

Elliott lay down on the bench, and Salvatore told him where to put his hands and showed him how far to lower the bar and then to bring it back up.

"Try for ten." Salvatore stood behind his head, his hands going up and down with the bar.

It wasn't too heavy, and Elliott did the ten reps pretty easily. What was hard was the way his gaze drew to Salvatore and how he looked standing behind him. Elliott clanged the bar back into the stops when he was done and sat up, smiling. "How many pounds is that?"

"Ninety-five. You did really good." Salvatore began adding plates to the bar and pumped out reps like it was nothing. Elliott simply watched as his shirt grew even tighter, the fabric straining against his muscles. When it was Elliott's turn, Salvatore changed out the plates on each end of the bar, and Elliott lifted again. This time, Salvatore helped him with the last few. "That was awesome, and it's just over a hundred pounds."

"So no more hundred-pound weakling," Elliott quipped.

Salvatore shook his head. "You've never done this before, and you did really well. It isn't about how much weight you push, but that you're making your muscles work a little, and you did that." He lightly patted Elliott on the back and took his turn.

They did a third set, then moved on to back exercises and then legs, shoulders, and arms.

"Is that all?" Elliott asked when they were done. His body felt a little different, but nothing hurt. "I thought there would be pain."

"'No pain, no gain' is bullshit," Salvatore told him. "If you feel pain, stop. That's never good. And you shouldn't hurt. That was a basic workout to get your muscles moving."

"That can't be what you do," Elliott said.

"No. I work specific muscle groups hard each day. But you could do what we did every other day and you'd get stronger. You could also do some cardio." Salvatore stopped as they were halfway to the locker room. "But you don't have to do anything. What Ivan said is right. You are cute, and…." He swallowed and seemed uncomfortable. "You don't need to change for anyone, certainly not for me. I just thought that if you were stronger, you might not be as afraid of your stepfather. Maybe if you want, I could work with you on self-defense or something."

"Do you know that sort of stuff?" Elliott liked that way Salvatore spoke to him, like he had a choice and could make his own decisions. There hadn't been many people in his life who actually thought that. His stepfather wanted to make all the decisions for everyone near him. He was the one in control, and everyone knew it. If you didn't, it was a lesson you learned very quickly.

"I have a fourth-degree black belt in karate. I earned that in the service. I used to teach classes as well, but I haven't done that in a while." Salvatore put his hand on Elliott's shoulder. "But it's up to you. There's no need to change or do this sort of thing to make me or anyone else happy. My goal is to make you feel better and more confident about yourself."

Elliott whistled. "Wow. I think that would be kind of cool." The idea that he could have some control over his own body and his own destiny was rather empowering.

"All right. Good." Once again Salvatore smiled. "Let's go clean up and then we can get something to eat. It isn't going to be too long before your appetite kicks in. There's a hot tub and a sauna. You can just wear the shorts if you want to bubble for a while. I recommend it to help relax your muscles." He went into the changing room, and Elliott followed.

He went to his locker and stripped down to the shorts before grabbing his towel and going through the bathroom and shower areas, finding his way to the pool and hot tub. The whirlpool was empty, and Elliott hung up his towel and then climbed into the warm water, found a seat, and leaned back to relax. He wasn't sure if Salvatore was going to come in as well, but got his answer when Salvatore hung up his towel and descended the steps into the water wearing only a small Speedo.

Damn, the man was gorgeous, with a ripped belly, thick arms, and a strong, plated chest. Elliott tried to keep his gaze north of the equator but failed, the bulge in the suit quite obvious. Thankfully, Salvatore sank into the water and settled a few feet away, stretching out his arms and relaxing. Elliott, on the other hand, was as tense as anything because he was just a short distance from him, and damn it all, he wanted to scoot over, plop his butt right into his lap, and hold on to him for dear life. Well, at least that was his momentary fantasy. Elliott kept his butt right where it belonged and hoped to hell he wasn't going to have to get up any time soon.

"You did really good."

"Thanks," Elliott said roughly. "It was fun."

"I know there are plenty of guys out there who can be intimidating and everything. But the reason to do this is to make yourself stronger and healthier. Exercise is a good thing. Just do something that you like to do. I walk on the treadmill on cardio days. I bring a book, walk, and read most times. It keeps the mind occupied, and I'll work out for an hour."

Elliott nodded. "What do you like to read?" He turned toward Salvatore. "I love adventure stories. As a kid, the *Harry Potter* books were a favorite. And I love the old Clive Cussler books. It was about the only thing I had in common with my stepfather. He had a set and I borrowed them. They were always so much fun. But they always got the girl, and I wanted to read stories where the hero got the boy." He smiled a little. "I wanted a book where a guy like me could get the hero and live happily ever after." Elliott shrugged. "Is that stupid?"

Salvatore shook his head.

"Anyway, then I found the Nightrunner series. It has two male protagonists who become lovers, and I read them all. They're great books and so much fun. I also saw myself in Seregil. He was sort of like me in that he didn't exactly fit in." Elliott settled back in the water and figured he should give Salvatore a chance to talk. "What about you?"

Salvatore smiled. "I love *Treasure*. It was my first Dirk Pitt novel, and I couldn't put it down."

"Me too. They're all pretty good, but some of them are better than others. I don't like the ones Cussler writes with other people. They aren't as good and often don't have that spark that the Dirk Pitt stories did." Elliott was getting warm, so he stood and sat on the edge of the tub, his legs dangling in the water. "It's pretty hot." He watched others swim laps in the pool and tried not to stare as the water bubbled around Salvatore's chest. "I think I'm going to go get showered." He checked the clock on the wall. "Bull is going to be expecting us soon, and I need to change and everything before I can go into work."

Salvatore stood and climbed out of the water, the suit hugging his muscled butt. Elliott swallowed and tried to remember the last time he had seen anyone who looked like him. Maybe in a catalog as a model, but not in real life.

Elliott got out himself, grabbed his towel, and followed Salvatore into the showers. He hung up his towel, took an empty shower, and pulled the curtain. It didn't take him long to clean up, and when he was done, he wrung out the shorts he'd worn as a suit, dried off, and wrapped the towel around his waist. He stepped out and nearly bumped into Ivan coming out of one of the other showers. "Sorry."

"It's okay, cutie," Ivan said with a gentle smile.

Elliott decided to ignore the comment. He headed into the locker room and changed into his clothes as quickly as he could. Salvatore wasn't out when he was done, so Elliott left the area and carried his things to the front of the club and took a seat in one of the chairs to wait.

Salvatore was right. His appetite had really kicked in, and his stomach growled. Thankfully he didn't have long to wait, and the two of them went out to the bike. Salvatore didn't say anything, and Elliott put on the helmet, stowed his bag, and got on behind him. They took off, and Salvatore drove even faster than he had getting there.

"ARE YOU angry about something?" Elliott asked when they pulled to a stop at a small restaurant a mile or so from the gym. Salvatore hadn't said anything, and his posture was as rigid as a pole.

"What did Ivan want?" Salvatore asked. "I heard him come on to you in the showers."

"I nearly bumped into him and said I was sorry." That was all there was to it as far as Elliott was concerned. "As for anything else, I think Ivan has a high opinion of himself. Maybe he's used to getting all the attention with his tan skin, big muscles, and intense eyes." He smiled. "But there's someone else I think I like more." Elliott was almost afraid to look at him. "He has these huge brown eyes and is really hot, and he's nice, and…." He tightened his hold on Salvatore's waist, even though they were standing still. Elliott leaned against Salvatore and held him a little tighter.

"Oh…."

"Were you jealous?" Elliott teased.

Salvatore sighed. "Maybe a little. I saw the way he kept looking at you the entire time we were in the gym. Like you were the main course at an all-you-can-eat buffet."

Elliot released Salvatore and climbed off the bike. "Ivan is probably a nice guy, but I get the feeling he's a 'wham, bam, bye' kind of guy. Once he gets what he wants, he moves on." That wasn't what Elliott wanted. "Let's go in and eat. I'm starved." He took off the helmet and waited for Salvatore to join him, and then they went inside.

"Was Ivan really watching me?" Elliott had been completely oblivious because his attention had been on what he was doing or on Salvatore.

"Yeah," Salvatore growled.

"That's so funny. I never even noticed." Elliott shrugged. They took a table in the café and opened one of the menus from the table. "Do they have good sandwiches?"

"The best. Their prime rib sandwich is really good, and it comes with this horseradish sauce that I love."

Elliott's mouth watered, and he set down the menu. When the server came over, they both ordered the sandwich, with a salad on the side.

Salvatore's phone chimed, and he snatched it up, then handed it to Elliott.

"Elliott, Bull. Officer Tom just called. Roderick's attorneys persuaded the judge that he wasn't going to go anywhere, and they posted bail. He's out as of a few minutes ago."

"Crap…."

"That's both good and bad. Tom told me that the judge specified that he wasn't to come anywhere near the club or any of its employees. Tom sent over a copy of the order, so we can have him arrested immediately if he shows anywhere near you. But he is out of jail."

"Oh…." Elliott's appetite suddenly flew out the window. Maybe he should have gotten the hell out of town. But then again, he knew Salvatore was probably right. If he ran, he'd keep running, and he wanted to have a life of his own.

"Where are you now?"

"Salvatore and I are having lunch." He couldn't help looking around for anyone familiar.

"When you're finished, come on down to the club. We can talk there and figure out what's the best thing to do."

"Okay. I'll tell him. Thanks." Elliott ended the call and handed the phone back to Salvatore, relaying what Bull had told him. "Let's finish up and then we can go to the club." He sat back in his chair. "I'm tired of feeling like a fucking scared rabbit all the time." It had been nice to not have to watch over his shoulder, even if it was for just a day.

"You shouldn't have to be."

Their drinks arrived, and a few minutes later, their food. Elliott refused to let Roderick or his stepfather take away his appetite, and he ate heartily. The food was as good as promised, and it wasn't long before both he and Salvatore had finished everything off.

"What time did Bull say to be there?"

"He said to come right down as soon as we were done." Elliott sat back and tried not to think about what he was going to do. Up until now he had been somewhat evasive about what had happened and what he'd seen, but he was going to have to tell someone everything. Once he did that, there would be no going back. His stepfather would have very little choice but to come after him in a big way. Elliott pulled out his wallet and handed the server the cash for their food. "Let's go. We need to get this over with."

"Anything you say," Salvatore teased.

They got on the bike once again and rode the rest of the way back to Salvatore's, where they took care of their wet stuff and Elliott changed for work. When they left again, they took Salvatore's car and drove back to the club.

CHAPTER 4

THE BACK door was open, and they went inside, where Spook met them, closed the door, and flipped the lock behind them.

"This is a private meeting, and Bull and I want you to know that whatever you tell us here will stay here. He and I are not, and have never been, cops." Spook's expression was as serious as death.

"Thanks." Elliott followed Spook out to the main floor of the club, where Bull sat at one of the tables, with a couple of unopened waters in front of him. Elliott sat down, and Bull handed him a bottle while the others sat as well. Salvatore took one and sat next to Elliott, feeling the nervous energy washing over him.

"What do you want to tell us?" Bull asked. "I have a ton of questions. I did some research into your stepfather, and I have to say that he is one nasty piece of work. Cloaks himself in respectability while he's dealing in some serious shit out the back door."

"That's my stepfather," Elliott said softly.

"What I don't understand is that you say your mother isn't aware of it," Spook said.

Bull's eyes widened. "There's no way that's true. His wife's name is all over his business dealings. It seems he hides some of his activities behind her name and her signatures."

Elliott swayed in the chair, and Salvatore gently touched his shoulder. "God, so bringing down my stepfather is going to do the same thing to my mother," he whispered, barely loud enough to be heard. "What the hell am I going to do?"

Bull leaned over the table, getting Elliott's attention. "Look, if your mother knows what's going on, then your stepfather sending someone to bring you home is also her doing it." He tapped Elliott's hand. "Your stepfather is the one law enforcement suspects. They

47

don't care about your mother unless she's willing to sell him up the river." Bull nodded. "What is it that you saw?"

"I didn't see anything at first, but I was in the house and I came down because I needed some paper for the printer in my room. My stepfather had some in his office." Elliott paused as if searching for the words. "God, I don't even know what to call him anymore. He used to be stepdad, but I can't call a snake in the grass that. It hurts too much."

"You can call him 'that bastard' if you like," Salvatore offered, and Elliott smiled a little and chuckled slightly.

"Well, anyway, I went to that bastard's office, and I heard him talking about a shipment coming in from Detroit that Roderick was to have someone pick up. It didn't take long for me to figure out it was drugs. At least that's what I thought, but it wasn't. It was a shipment—more like a load—of weapons. He had arranged for them to be shipped across the border, and then they were to be 'stolen.' The plan was for a hundred thousand dollars in guns to turn into a million overnight. They could easily be sold for so much more on the street, where no one could trace them." Elliott slowly rocked from side to side.

"What did you do?" Bull asked and Salvatore took his hand to lend support and let him know that he was there for him.

"I went back toward my room, and when I heard someone coming toward me, I pretended to be coming to see the fucking bastard. I asked him some stupid questions and then got the hell out of there."

Bull nodded. "That explains part of what you heard, but…."

"I couldn't leave well enough alone. Not by a long shot. Not me. That night, after the house was quiet, maybe about two or so, I went back down to the office. Long ago I had found out where the bastard kept the keys to his files, and I unlocked the drawers and found the shipment details. I copied them, along with a bunch more of his records. I should have been more careful about how I put things back. He was ranting and raving about how his files had been rummaged through a few days later. By then I had hidden my copies well, but it was a matter of time before he figured out it was me, so I got the hell out of dodge and came here. That was a month ago."

Salvatore leaned closer. "What did you live on?"

"I closed out some of my bank accounts and took what I had in cash. That was what I used to pay for everything. I didn't take my credit cards or even my phone. I left them all there. I took a cab to the train station and bought a ticket to New York, but got off here. I thought I could try to put them off. But they must have traced me somehow."

Salvatore hated the defeated expression in Elliott's eyes. There had been such determination just a little while ago, and now it seemed like it was gone.

"It's very hard to disappear today," Bull said calmly. "With the way we're connected and the internet. Your stepfather could have hired a PI to do a skip trace, and most of the time they barely need to leave their computer any longer. A name on a utility bill, or the smallest slipup, is enough to trigger what they need."

Elliott grew pale. "I didn't think about that. I bet the landlord transferred the utilities to me and… I was trying to be so careful." He groaned and hung his head.

"Don't you worry about it. Even professionals have a hard time falling off the grid," Salvatore said, and Bull nodded his agreement.

"He's right," Bull said, then pulled the conversation back to where he wanted it. "Where are all the papers you copied?"

"I have them in a safe-deposit box in Pittsburgh. I put them there before I left. It's in my name, but I made sure that only I have access to it."

"Are the keys in your apartment?" Bull asked, speaking faster.

"No." Elliott reached into his pocket and pulled out a ring with keys on it. "I wasn't sure where to put them, so I kept them with me."

"I suggest you wear one of them close to your skin. Maybe on a chain around your neck, under your clothes. You can put the other in the safe here if you'd like," Bull offered, and Elliott gave him one of the keys, which he handed to Spook to take care of.

Elliott finished his water and closed his eyes. "I'm not sure what to do going forward."

They all remained quiet for a full thirty seconds, and then Bull broke the silence. "What sort of information do you have in those papers? Did you look at them all?"

Elliott shook his head. "I found the information on the guns, but I copied all the papers I could. There has to be a couple hundred pages. But I was tired and I didn't want to get caught, so I stopped and put things away. The copy machine is in his office, and I didn't want it to be warm when he came in early the next morning, so I took what I had and got out. When he got so mad and started scouring for who had been in his office, I opened the safe-deposit box account, got what cash I could, and left town."

"So there could be anything in there?" Bull asked.

"It was mostly shipping manifests and things like that, but there was other stuff too. I just copied as much as I could." Elliott sighed. "Maybe I should have just left well enough alone and kept my eyes down and my mouth shut."

"Why did you do it?" Salvatore asked quietly.

Elliott turned toward him. "Because when my mom married him, he was nice enough. I was thirteen, and he used to take me places and we did things together. It was fun, like having a real dad once again. It had been just Mom and me for four years after my father died. Then she met that bastard, and everything was good for a while. Once they got married, he changed. I saw it pretty fast. He tried to control her and me. We moved into his big house, and he had more security installed. He said it was because he wanted to keep us safe, but soon enough we couldn't leave without him knowing, and then I had to ask permission." Elliott's hands closed around the empty bottle, clutching it tightly. "When I graduated high school, he tried to pick the college I went to. I applied to a lot of places, but I found my applications in the trash in his office. Then he was mad when I didn't get in." Elliott wiped his face. "I hated him for that. But I was stuck there, except for when I went to work."

"Had you been looking for something to get even with your stepfather?" Bull asked, and Elliott shook his head.

"Did you just want to get out?" Salvatore clarified.

"Yeah. That's what I wanted. But I was scared and had no idea how to get away. Then I heard all that stuff and I knew that he had a vulnerability, so I copied all I could. I know he knows it was me, or he's pretty sure I was the one in his office, but if I had stayed, I'd have either been locked up in the house or my mom would be planning my funeral." Elliott quivered like a leaf, and Salvatore put an arm around his shoulders.

"It's okay. He must know that you haven't turned the papers over to anyone or he'd have investigators by the dozen at his door armed with search warrants and arrest papers. Which also explains why he sent someone to bring you back. He needs to know what you've done and what you have."

"Yes," Bull agreed, then smiled. "He has to be shitting bricks wondering what's going to happen."

"That and he'll cover as many of his tracks as he possibly can. Records will be burned, and anyone who knows anything is probably going to start to disappear. If he can get his hands on me, then I'll be the one who will never be seen again. I know that now." Elliott leaned against him, and Salvatore tightened his hold on him. "I don't know what to do."

Bull sat quietly, and Salvatore thought as well before offering a suggestion. "We could go to Pittsburgh and retrieve those papers. If they are explosive, we turn them over to the police and let them handle the whole thing." It seemed simple enough, but Salvatore knew nothing was that cut and dried.

"Yes, we could," Bull agreed halfheartedly. "Banking records are confidential, but that doesn't mean he won't have someone try to see if you have an account there." He paused. "But before we do anything, we'd better know as much about your stepfather as we can."

"Like what?" Elliott asked even as Salvatore nodded. *Know as much about your enemy as possible.*

"What are his weaknesses?" Salvatore asked. "Where is he vulnerable? Does he like women? Boys? Does he gamble? What are his vices?"

"Does he have a regular routine?" Bull asked. "Something he does every day or every week? Those can be used to our advantage. If he has a routine, then we know where he's going to be and we can either avoid him or we can meet him… antagonize him. Maybe interrupt his business enough that he realizes we're going to make his life more miserable than he can make yours. I'm not saying we'll do that, but I want you to get the idea. The more info we have, the better."

"Okay, ummm." Elliott sighed. "He once had a fit that I put a family picture on Facebook and made me take it down. He tried to make me close the account, but I just left it instead."

"Is it still there? A picture would be a good place to start." Salvatore brought up the app on his phone and handed it to Elliott. "See if you can find it."

Elliott scrolled through. "I was mad at him, so I hid the post, but I didn't delete the picture."

He handed the phone back, and Salvatore stared at the picture of a man with salt-and-pepper hair and glasses, in tan slacks and a polo shirt. He looked like someone's grandfather. Next to him was a woman with blonde hair the same color as Elliott's. It could only be his mother. They were together, but it wasn't a posed picture. The two of them were talking to someone else barely in the image.

"I'm going to pull the image, and I'll send it to all of you." He got busy and then forwarded it around.

"Any routines?" Bull prompted, but Elliott shook his head. "What about vices?"

"His vice is money in any and all forms. It doesn't matter how much he has, he wants more," Elliott said.

"Greed," Bull muttered. "Is he faithful to your mom?"

Elliott shrugged. "He never took me to titty bars or things like that. I've never known him to have women or even flirt at a party." He stiffened. "Why?"

"Because if we can find proof that he has been unfaithful, maybe that will undermine your mother's support. Even if we have evidence that can be used against him, your mother can't be compelled to testify. But maybe she will if she learns that he's a cheating scum," Bull explained. "No one likes to be made a fool of."

"True…," Elliott said cautiously, as though something were tickling the back of his mind.

"What is it?"

"We were out to dinner for Mom's birthday last year and a woman approached the table. Mom turned to say something to the bastard, touching his arm, and the woman backed away quickly." He scratched his head. "It could be nothing."

"Mistress," Spook said. "Classic behavior. She saw your father and came over to say hello, but then saw your mother and backed away. Pretty simple to figure out that she knows about your mom. I'll check it out. See what I can find out from my contacts."

"But don't let anyone know that we're interested or why. Be discreet," Bull said.

"Always am," Spook said without heat. "While I'm at it, I'll check on his financial dealings. See if there's anything hidden in plain sight." He stepped closer, and they both shifted their gazes to him. "I don't want to be a dick here, but are you prepared to find out things you might not want to know? It's possible your mom is actually involved… or that your stepfather is into things that are going to make you squeamish as hell." His expression was almost gentle. "Just prepare yourself so you aren't too shocked."

"I'll try. But how can you prepare yourself to find out that your stepfather is a gangster and that your mother is a moll?" Elliott rolled his eyes. "This is all a little too much."

"Sometimes the truth sucks," Salvatore said.

Spook nodded. "And sometimes it's liberating as anything." Spoken like a man who knew exactly what he was talking about. "Now, how do we keep Elliott safe? There are going to be people looking for him, and they already know that he works here. The club is going to be point central for anyone trying to find him."

"That means that we need to be on our toes. If we see anyone, we take action first. We can apologize if we're wrong, but I want this place to be a fortress. We search everyone, not just for alcohol, but for weapons. And we check all IDs. Tell the men at the door that anyone with a western PA license is suspicious and they need to inform one of us." Bull's eyes grew hard as stone. "And if anyone so much as thinks of taking a tip to let someone in, I will kick them to the curb so fast their ass will have boot prints that last for a week."

"Got it," Salvatore and Spook said at the same time.

"We need to tell the bartenders that anyone looking for info or asking questions is to be pointed out, and questions are to be deflected. I don't care how innocuous they might seem. This place is going to be fucking Fort Knox. I don't want any trouble, and we're going to assume that anything out of the ordinary is trouble. It's Saturday night, the busiest night of the week, so we are going to be on our toes." Bull turned to Elliott and gentled his expression. "I don't want you to stay until closing. Once the crowd begins to thin out, Salvatore is going to take you home. Use the back and don't make a fuss. By a little after one, the floor usually begins to thin, and you can go then."

Elliott nodded. "Of course, if that's what you want. But that isn't fair to everyone else who has to stay to clean up and prepare for the next day."

"It's Sunday and we're closed. There will be a few people in to do the weekly cleaning anyway. I don't want you in the club when we close. If there are a lot of people around, then you have some cover and it will be harder for anyone watching the club to pick you out. After two in the morning, we're pretty easy to spot on the street."

"What do you want him to do if he spots someone he knows?" Salvatore asked. He was concerned that they put something in place, some signal.

"Spook and I will be on the floor at all times. And you will be in charge at the doors. Hank is going to be behind the bar. I'll speak to him, but all you need to do is get any of us. If you can't see Spook or me, go to Hank right away. He's always behind the bar, and you have regular contact with him. Salvatore, if you have any suspicions at the door, you're to call either of us. Basically, we all back each other up and stay alert." Bull looked at each of them, and they all nodded.

"Then I should probably get things started and ready for opening," Elliott said, standing up and starting to lower the chairs to the floor.

"He needs to keep busy," Salvatore said softly.

"We'll watch for any trouble in the club. You do your best to keep it from getting in the door." Bull stood and pushed his chair under the table, then gathered up the bottles. Hank arrived, and he and Bull spent some time behind the bar, probably going over what they had discussed, as well as what they could expect for the night.

Salvatore got everything set at the door to handle cover charges and reviewed the evening's procedures with all the guys, as well as Bull's no-tip rule.

"You have to be kidding me," one of the guys, Hugo, groused. "How are we supposed to make any money?"

"You aren't supposed to be taking tips to let people in at all," Salvatore explained. "That ends now, and if you aren't happy about that"—he pointed to the street—"there's the road." He wasn't going to take that kind of graft happening from anyone.

Hugo actually thought about it, and Salvatore was moments from firing the guy outright, except he wanted to talk to Bull first. He would when he got the chance, and maybe they would need to hire someone else in the end anyway. "Fine."

"If I see anything, you're gone. That goes for all of you. This is a business, and Bull sets the rules. We aren't supposed to be making deals or lining our own pockets, ever." He started to tell all of them he wasn't playing games. "Now, there have been rumors that local drug gangs are going to try to get in to deal."

"No way," Hugo said. "That shit gives us all a bad name."

Well, at least some of his talk might have gotten through.

"Then we all need to be vigilant. Check for weapons, as well as anyone trying to carry in. If in doubt, ask people to stand to the side. Bull or I will deal with them. We can call the police if needed, but we don't need to confront anyone or put ourselves in any danger."

"What about the smart-mouths?"

Salvatore knew exactly what he was talking about. "This is a private establishment, and no one has a God-given right to get in. If protestors show up, they can protest across the street if they wish." A few groups had tried to protest right in front of the club a few months ago, and the patrons had pretty much squeezed them off the sidewalk and out into the street. It was a beautiful thing. A few of the drag queens had even strode up and had pictures taken with them. That had unnerved the protestors more than anything else. "Are there any more questions?"

No one said anything, so Salvatore set the men up at the door. Since it was Saturday, they usually opened a little earlier. The music began and the lighting lowered, lasers and strobes starting. Salvatore unlocked the door, and the guys started the search process with the first few patrons.

The front door grew busier as the hours passed. Salvatore was able to check on Elliott a few times to make sure that he was okay and that he hadn't seen anyone familiar in the club. As of about nine, everything was going just fine. They had busted a few guys for trying to carry in liquor and sent them on their way. One guy had a knife, and he was told he could check it or leave. He left as well. Sometimes it struck Salvatore just how dumb some people were and what they would try to get away with.

"Salvatore?" Hugo said, getting his attention and pointing toward a guy who seemed very uncomfortable as he stood in line.

"I see him. When he gets to the front of the line, I'll handle him."

The more Salvatore watched him and the way he moved, the more he was certain this guy was suspicious. Most of the guys in line talked to the people around them, excitedly waiting to get inside. This guy looked like it was as enjoyable a prospect as pulling teeth. He kept trying to turn into himself, and looked around nervously, probably to see if he was recognized. It was almost painful to watch, and part of Salvatore got a perverse pleasure out of it.

When the man reached the front, Salvatore patted him down as he tried to stay sharp and keep his heart from running the hell away.

He expected to find a gun or a weapon, but there was nothing. The man nearly jumped out of his skin as soon as Salvatore touched him, though.

He met the man's eyes. "You don't belong here," he said without threatening him, but that much was clear.

"You all need to repent," the man said, finally finding his voice.

"And you need to stop being so damned nervous. You're going to wet yourself." Salvatore chuckled and motioned to the side as his heart rate slowed back to normal. This guy wasn't here for Elliott. "You have a good night and move on."

"But…." He pulled out his money.

"You can do your preaching and proselytizing someplace else. Now quietly move on." Salvatore motioned and puffed up a little, and the man headed on down the street, probably not wanting the trouble.

"That was interesting," Hugo said from next to him.

"Yeah. That happens every now and then." Salvatore turned to the others. "The thing is to kill them with kindness. They aren't going to get in, so just be nice about it and they have nothing to fight against." He turned as the man got into a car and drove away. "Keep an eye out." He had a feeling something was going to happen… and when they least expected it.

THE FRONT door ran smoothly all night. There were plenty of people wanting to get in, including a bachelorette party.

"Why come here?" Salvatore asked the bride with a smile. He was just a little curious.

She grinned. "The guys are nice, they know how to dance, they look good, and we don't have to worry about being hit on. It's the perfect place. And I want to have some fun."

They weren't wearing all that much, so it was easy enough to see that they weren't hiding anything. Still, he checked over each of the ladies and let them inside with a bemused smile and a notion that the evening just got a little rowdier than they'd expected.

"We've got this here," Hugo said. He had really changed his tune since their earlier talk. "Go check that everything is okay inside."

Salvatore met his gaze, trying to see if he was up to something.

"Don't worry. I heard what you said, loud and clear." He nodded, and Salvatore went inside.

The club was hopping, that was for sure. He looked over the crowd to check for trouble and to see if he could find Elliott. It took a few minutes, but then he came through his line of sight on his way to the bar. Salvatore tilted his head, and Elliott came over. "Is everything okay? No issues?"

"Nothing out of the ordinary. Just a guy who couldn't keep his hands to himself." Elliott turned to a table where a guy dabbed at his clothes with a napkin. "He wanted a glass of water, and some of it spilled all over his lap. That should cool him off."

"You didn't…," Salvatore said.

"No, I didn't. One of his tablemates did the honors—I just got to witness the glorious bit of karma." Elliott smiled. "Is everything okay for you? No issues?"

"None worth worrying about." Salvatore had been hoping that something would happen. The waiting and expecting some sort of move kept him on his toes, but not knowing if it was coming or not was nerve-racking. "Keep your eyes open, and we'll do the same." He squeezed Elliott's hand and then released it again. "I need to get back."

"I'll call if I see anything."

"Me too." God, Salvatore wanted to step forward, wrap Elliott in his arms, kiss him within an inch of his life, and make sure he was safe forever. Maybe take him home and keep him behind locked doors so no one could hurt him. But Elliott wasn't his, and it would be a shame to lock away someone as amazing as him. His heart hurt at the thought, just like his blood raced whenever his mind turned to the fact that someone was after him. Salvatore smiled and tried to put down the images his mind conjured up of Elliott in the whirlpool, only in his mind, they were alone and Elliott's bathing suit suddenly slipped down past his hips and….

Salvatore pulled his thoughts back to the present and told Elliott he'd see him later before returning to the front door.

The club filled up by eleven, and after that, the line barely moved. They had to wait for people to leave before letting others in. It was the time of night when tempers flared and patience ran thin. Some guys left rather than wait, while a few others tried to muscle or even pay their way in.

"You need to wait with the others," Salvatore told a man in his early thirties when he approached him.

The man pulled some bills from his pocket and peeled off a couple of hundreds. "There's someone inside that I'm supposed to meet." His voice was smooth, and his eyes were filled with confidence.

"I see." Salvatore took the bills, handed them to Hugo, and checked his identification, all the while his suspicions rising. Then he asked the man to stand still while he patted him down. "It must be some meeting." He snatched the knife from his waist. "Is this the kind of thing you really take to meet someone?" Salvatore raised his eyebrows as he held the man in place. "Get Bull," he told Hugo, who ducked inside immediately.

"What's all this about?" The guy tried to pull away, but Salvatore held him in place until Spook joined them.

"I found him first," Hugo said as Spook charged up to the man Salvatore held.

"Carson," Spook said, calmly.

"You know him?" Salvatore asked.

"Yes. You can let him go," Spook said. "He isn't going to try anything… at least not now." Spook held Carson's gaze, and he nodded. "Come inside. I think we need to talk."

Carson nodded. "It would seem so."

"You too, Salvatore," Spook added.

Salvatore made sure the guys had the door and followed Spook inside and around the dancing mob of guys—where he noticed that the bridal party seemed to be having the time of their lives—to the back-room area.

"You should get Elliott."

"He should be going on break." Salvatore was already signaling him at the bar. Elliott held up two fingers and took his tray of drinks toward his tables. Salvatore waited for him to finish. "Is it break time?"

"God yes," Elliott said.

Salvatore pointed toward the office. Instantly Elliott's posture stiffened, but he walked ahead of him, the music from the club shutting off as soon as the door closed behind them.

The small security office was just inside the door, built as part of the latest renovations. "What's going on?" Elliott asked. Spook and Bull sat across from Carson. Elliott didn't react to him, and looked at Bull and Spook.

"This is Carson," Spook said calmly. "He and I have a history together. Most of it pretty good, which is sort of a miracle.'

"Lowell here saved my life once." Carson turned back to Spook. "So, what are you doing here? This can't be a coincidence. Did this job get contracted twice?"

"Spook is the head of security for the club. He's been on the staff for a couple of years now," Bull explained. "He isn't in the business any longer. Hasn't been for a while." He seemed surprisingly relaxed as he reached across the table. "Bull Krebs."

Carson whistled. "Okay. So, I stepped into old friends week or something."

"Maybe a little. Look, we want to know why you're here. You mentioned a job. What is it and who hired you?" Spook got right down to business.

"Was it my stepfather?" Elliott asked as he approached the table. He and Salvatore took the last two seats in the room.

Carson turned to Elliott, then reached into his light jacket, pulled out a picture, and laid it on the table. It was definitely Elliott.

"What were you supposed to do?" Spook asked. "What was the job?"

"What was the knife for?" Salvatore pressed.

Spook turned to him. "It's his weapon of choice. Carson could throw his knife across the dance floor out there, through a damned crowd, and only hit the person he wanted." He turned back to Carson as Elliott paled, and Salvatore steadied him so he didn't fall out of his chair. "I think it's time to lay the cards on the table," Spook said. "No games, just the truth."

"I don't know who hired me. The job came through my agent. All cash, paid in advance. I was to bring home my target. I got a bonus if he was alive, but it wasn't necessary." He spoke so matter-of-factly, and Salvatore wanted to beat the living shit out of the guy.

"And this is the kind of work you do?" Salvatore asked.

Carson turned to him. "Yeah, the world is one sick place." He shifted his attention to Spook. "You know how these jobs go. You take it, you do it, and you turn off your emotions. Whatever you think or feel doesn't matter. I'm sure Elliott is a nice guy, and whoever paid for the job is—"

"A total piece of shit," Salvatore said.

"Yeah, we know the drill. But now we have a problem. You aren't going to complete your contract. That's the price. You owe me one, and I'm collecting. Just walk away."

Carson nodded. "You know I will. But what about the next guy? And there will be another. That's how these things work. I'll return the money, but someone else is likely going to take it."

Salvatore jumped to his feet. "This is an innocent person, you know that? It's his rotten stepfather who's trying to get him." His temper couldn't handle any more.

"Okay. I get that, and I can also understand that you care for the guy. But facts are facts, and I can't alter them just because I have a change of heart. I'm telling you, all of you, what's going to happen."

"Salvatore, please sit back down," Elliott said. "Is there any way you can find out who actually paid you? I know there's probably stuff in place to keep things secret, but could you find out?"

"Probably," Carson said.

"Then do so," Spook told him. "You're involved now, whether you like it or not. This job just turned into a clusterfuck for you. But we need your help." Spook leaned over the table. "I know you, and I know why you do what you do."

"Don't... talk... about it," Carson hissed.

"No. That's your business. We all have our reasons for doing this shit, but there comes a time for all of us when the cost is too great. When we run the danger of losing our soul." Spook spoke like someone who knew exactly what he was talking about.

"You have to have one to lose it," Carson said, putting up his hands. "Look." He turned to Elliott, who was still pale. "I'll do what I can to help you get proof of who's behind this. I owe Spook a favor and I pay my debts. But I don't know what else I can do to help you."

"Maybe give us a couple of days. Stall for some time, find out what you can. At least it will give us a chance to get to the bottom of this and see if we can't figure out a way to make this all end," Spook said.

"But it doesn't seem to matter. I'm never going to be able to just live my life. This is going to follow me forever. My bastard stepfather is going to hound me until I'm dead or living the rest of my life under his control." There was a hint of panic in Elliott's voice.

"That's what we're all trying to see doesn't happen." Salvatore tried to soothe him, but probably wasn't successful. "You have plenty of people in your corner, including all of us… well, except this Carson guy, but it seems even he's going to help. You have to keep your head and not panic. That's when you get into trouble." He took Elliott's hand, trying to comfort him, but all he got was nerves from him. Not that Salvatore blamed him. This sort of thing wasn't really something people usually thought about.

Carson stood. "Look, I'm out of this. I'll stall as long as I can, then return the money and see what information I can get. But I can't find out anything until after I return the cash." He didn't seem happy, but it appeared the debt he owed Spook was worth more than he was being paid. That was probably the only reason he was backing away. "I'm going to leave you all to your strategy session, and I'll be in touch with Spook in a few days." He went for the door, and Spook left along with him.

Elliott still seemed about ready to fall out of his chair. "What about bringing the fight to my stepfather? Could we put a hit out on h m? He has to have a ton of enemies. If he's done the things I think he has, then there are enemies galore."

"I don't think so," Bull said. "Getting someone to take care of you is a pretty low-risk, quick kind of job. I'm not being harsh, just truthful. Taking out someone like Antonio Losquaro is going to take a lot more money than any of us has. Not that there are many people who would be willing to take on that kind of job in the first place, regardless of the money offered." Bull drummed his fingers on the top of the table. "But I understand what you're thinking. Right now, he's the one bringing it, and that puts us at his mercy. There has to be a way to take the fight to him."

Salvatore nodded. "How do we do that?"

"I'm not sure. You need to keep Elliott safe until we can figure something out." Bull stood. "I have to go back out there. Elliott, do you want to finish your shift? You can stay in here if you want."

Elliott shook his head. "I'm not going to make a living if I sit back here. I need to work." He sighed and straightened his clothes. Then he left the room, with Salvatore behind.

Bull stopped him at the door. "I'll watch the front. You keep an eye on him out there." He went to leave after Salvatore nodded.

"Bull," Salvatore said, and Bull stopped. "Elliott keeps asking why everyone is doing this for him, and I don't think my answers are sufficient."

Bull shrugged. "Because it's the right thing to do. And that's enough for me. I can't speak for anyone else, but I'm doing this because I have done more jobs like Carson's in my career and I have plenty to atone for. Being on the side of right is enough." Bull turned and passed through the door to the club. Salvatore did the same, Bull's words ringing in his ears as he tried to find Elliott in the crowd of people.

SALVATORE WATCHED the crowd for the rest of the night. He scrutinized everyone who got close to Elliott, but there was no further excitement, at least as far as Elliott was concerned. Salvatore did break up a few altercations and escorted two men out of the club for dealing. They ultimately departed in police cars. Bull didn't put up with that sort of activity at all.

"It's my lunchtime," Elliott said when he approached him after midnight.

"All right."

Elliott took him by the hand and tugged him out onto the floor. "Bull said it was your break time too." Elliott shimmied his backside, his hips undulating in small fluid circles that left Salvatore's mouth dry. "Come on, dance with me. Just for a few minutes." He pulled Salvatore close and moved against him. Salvatore had no idea how to dance. It was one of the things he'd never learned to do. Still, Elliott made him want things he hadn't before, so he did his best to mirror his movements. Salvatore thought he probably looked like an uncoordinated duck, but with the way Elliott looked at him, with heat and passion in his eyes, Salvatore didn't care how he looked to anyone other than Elliott.

"You're beautiful," Salvatore said.

Elliott reached up and wound his arms around Salvatore's neck, pressing to him. And damned if that wasn't an amazing feeling. Salvatore enclosed Elliott's waist in his arms, holding him tighter, letting Elliott guide him as the music and the heat from Elliott's body threatened to overwhelm his senses.

Time seemed to disconnect from him. Salvatore lost track of how long they were out there together until the song came to an end and the beat changed. He stepped back, and Elliott's hands slipped away.

"I have to get back to work. Ummm… thank you." He smiled and Salvatore returned it.

"You're an amazing dancer." He stroked Elliott's cheek, wishing they had more time for just the two of them, but duty called. Salvatore took a step back and watched as Elliott turned and strode toward the bar, going back to work. Salvatore moved out of the crush of dancers to the edge of the dance floor, watching the others even as his gaze was drawn to Elliott.

Salvatore needed to get his head where it belonged so he could help protect Elliott, but it was hard. Every time Elliott's gaze found him across the dance floor, Salvatore's heart beat a little faster and sweat broke out on the back of his neck.

A tap on his shoulder pulled him back to the present, and he turned. Zach, Bull's husband, looked up at him. "I swear we need to hire some short bouncers. I'm tired of having to look up at all of you. Sometimes my neck hurts." He rubbed the back and then laughed. "You know it's okay if you like Elliott. He's a nice guy."

"I see," Salvatore said. "Are you playing matchmaker? Spook warned me that you have that tendency." He shook his head.

"No, I'm not." Zach pointed. "I was coming over to tell you that that guy over there bought Elliott a drink and I think he put something in it." He glared for a split second. "And, okay, maybe I was trying to fix you up a little. But it seems you don't need me. Go save Elliott." He waved him off, and Salvatore hurried over to where the patron was about to offer Elliott a drink.

Salvatore was pretty sure Elliott would turn it down, but it was superhot in here tonight, and his concern for Elliott made his heart beat faster. Even he might be tempted to down something cool, in some sort of momentary lapse of judgment. "Elliott." He fixed a glare at the men at the table. "I think these gentlemen have had enough this evening and will be leaving." He turned to the men. "I saw what you tried to do. Now, you can settle your tab and go now, or I'll have the police come, they can test this drink, and then you can answer all their questions about what they will find in it." All three of them paled, and the guy closest to him pulled out his wallet and laid some bills on the table. The others did the same, and then they left in a damn hurry.

"What are you talking about? They offered me the Coke I brought." Elliott huffed.

"Zach saw them drug it," Salvatore told him. "And I know it's against the rules, but as hot as it is in here, I didn't want you to drink it." The thought of Elliott being at someone else's mercy made his blood boil.

"I wasn't. I would have thanked them and taken the drink back to the bar. Hank would have given me a replacement." Elliott touched his cheek. "But thank you for watching out for me." A tear ran down his cheek, and Salvatore brushed it away. "I don't know how much more of this I can take. All of it. The whole thing is almost too much."

"What's going on?" Grant asked, his gaze alternating between them.

"Someone tried to give Elliott a spiked drink," Salvatore explained. "He's okay."

Grant's gaze softened immediately. "Are you sure? You didn't drink any of it, did you?" He sighed and fanned himself as Elliott shook his head. "Go get yourself something to drink. I'm going to see if I can fix this." Grant fanned himself once again. "I think I'm going to pass out, it's so warm." He hurried away, and a minute later, blessed cool air slowly descended from the ceiling.

"I understand wanting it warm so people will drink, but this is a bit much." Elliott sighed and stood still. "Dang, that feels good."

"Are you really okay?" Salvatore asked yet again. He wanted to take Elliott aside and check him over just to be sure. But he didn't have any right to do that.

"Yes. I didn't drink any of it."

Salvatore gently gripped Elliott's shoulders and leaned closer. "I know that. I mean, are you going to be okay? All this is hard enough on anyone. Hell, I'm trained to deal with stress and this is getting to me." He rubbed gently.

"I'm okay. I'll probably fall to pieces after work, but right now I have things I have to do." Elliott half smiled, and Salvatore released him. Elliott turned and went back to work, while Salvatore looked after him. Then he sighed and went to get his head back in the game himself.

"ARE YOU sure that no one is out there?" Elliott asked at the back door of the club.

"I checked. No one is around, and I have the guys in front watching the street entrance, so no one is going to be able to get in either." There was little Salvatore could do about the other two buildings that had doors that opened onto the space. But they were for emergencies only, and he had never seen them used. Still, he kept his gaze peeled for any sort of threat until they got in the car. Then they were on the road to the house, with Salvatore taking a roundabout route in case they were followed.

He pulled right into the garage once he got them home, leaving the engine running. Then he sighed and let go of some of the tension. "I'm going to check out the house. You slide over and get out of here if anything happens. Don't worry or wait for me. Just go." He handed Elliott his phone. "Call Bull if you have to and tell him what happened. He'll know exactly what to do." Salvatore got out and went inside.

Everything seemed normal, and nothing had been touched. He checked his indicators, and none of the doors had been opened. Retracing his steps, Salvatore opened the back garage door and motioned for Elliott to come inside.

Once Elliott closed the garage door and turned off the car engine, Salvatore locked the back door behind them and switched on more lights. "Are you hungry?"

Elliott shook his head. "The last thing I want is food. My stomach feels like it's going to punish me for the rest of my life." His legs seemed wobbly, and he sat down. "To think that my stepfather hates me enough to want me killed." He closed his eyes and breathed deeply. "I guess that just goes to show the kind of man he really is." Elliott raised his gaze. "Part of me hoped that I was wrong and that I…." He swallowed and put his arms on the table, resting his head on them. "I don't quite know how to deal with this."

Salvatore could easily understand that. He gently stroked Elliott's shoulders until he sat back up. Then he tugged Elliott to his feet, lifted him into his arms, and carried him down the hall to the bedroom. "It's okay. You just need some time to process what's happening." He toed open the door to Elliott's bedroom and laid him on the bed.

"What are you doing?"

"I'm putting you in the bed so you can rest. It's late and there's been a lot going on. You need to try to sleep and let your mind get a handle on this, so I thought—" His words cut off when Elliott kissed him. It was gentle at first, but as soon as he responded, Elliott held him tighter, deepening the kiss until Elliott grew nearly frantic, like a live wire.

"I…." Elliot gasped when they broke apart. "I need to feel alive and that everything is going to be all right." He began to shake, and as much as Salvatore would have loved to have been able to take Elliott to his bed and act on these new feelings that kept growing inside him, he knew it was best if he pulled back. This wasn't the way he wanted Elliott's and his first time.

"I know." Salvatore held Elliott's hands in his. "But is this out of fear?"

Elliott lowered his gaze. "I get it."

"Get what?" Salvatore said.

"You carried me in the bedroom…. I thought that was because you liked me, and…." He began breathing harder and faster. "I thought you wanted me." He wiped his eyes and jumped off the bed.

"I do. I think you're—"

Elliott shook his head as if to stop the words form reaching his ears.

"Look." Salvatore stood and hugged him, letting his fingers card through Elliott's hair. "All night long I couldn't take my eyes off you. No matter what. I should have been working, but I kept watching you."

"Then why?" Elliott was nearly crying, and Salvatore knew it was everything bubbling over all at once. He held Elliott tighter and let him release everything he'd been holding inside.

"Because I want you when you can think straight, okay?" Salvatore made small circles on Elliott's back. "Just take some deep breaths, relax, and let your head begin to clear. I'm not going anywhere, so just give yourself a chance to breathe and think about what's going on. Your head is going in a million different directions." He took a single step back. "I don't want you to wake up tomorrow morning and wonder what you've done." The truth was that if he did sleep with Elliott, it had to mean more than just a night of sex.

"Really?" Elliott asked.

"Yeah. You're a young guy. Me, I've been around, and I've seen shit that you don't want to even hear about, let alone witness." Salvatore sat on the edge of the bed, and Elliott eventually took the place next to him. "I've slept with guys and women because I had to in order to get the job done." He swallowed hard. This was the part of his past that he had worked hard to keep buried. Sometimes it came to him unbidden and at the worst possible times. "I don't want you to think that's why I'm interested. I like you. I really do."

"I think I see," Elliott said.

"Maybe and maybe not. It's hard for someone who hasn't seen the stuff I have or lived what I had to in order to survive. But I will tell you that when you and I do spend time together… like that, I want it to be special. Not because you're scared or because your head is going a million miles an hour." Salvatore sighed. "I know it may sound like the most *un*guy thing you've ever heard, but I want sex to mean something. It has to." He turned to Elliott. "And I want it to with you." Salvatore yawned. "I can't believe I told you some of that shit. I must be more tired than I thought." He lay back on the bed.

"You really did stuff like that? I thought it was only in the movies. James Bond kind of things." Elliott lay next to him.

"Nope. It happens. When you have a job to do and someone gets in the way, you fuck them, kill them, or put them somewhere they can't get to you until it's over. That was the kind of stuff I did. Black ops. You're sent by the government to clean up a mess, and if things go wrong, nobody knows nothing." Salvatore put his hands on the side of his head. "Maybe someday I'll tell you more, but so much of what I did is top secret." He closed his eyes, because even if it wasn't, he had learned a long time ago to treat it as if it were, just in case. "There has been so much deception, so much time spent fast and loose with the rules. I need something real, and I think that maybe you could be that something."

Elliott rolled onto his side, a hand sliding gently over his chest. "You really want to take your time?"

"Yeah, I do." Salvatore rolled over as well, sliding a leg between Elliott's and drawing him closer. "Let's give ourselves a chance. Anticipation is a wonderful thing, and I can wait for you." He leaned forward and kissed Elliott gently, savoring the slightly sweet taste of his lips. He didn't want to give Elliott the wrong idea or lead him on, so he pulled back with a sigh.

"Is that snack still available?" Elliott asked, sitting up.

"Sure." Salvatore sat and cleared his head of the Elliott haze. "I can make some eggs and toast. That should be easy enough." He checked the time, got off the bed, and went to the kitchen, where he got out the pan, put some bread in the toaster, and set about scrambling some eggs.

It was quick snack and tasted good. Elliott must have enjoyed it as well, because he cleaned his plate and finished his juice, then yawned broadly. Salvatore had to stifle his own yawn as he took care of the dishes and then went right to the bathroom to clean up. He wasn't sure if he should invite Elliott to sleep with him or not. The whole conversation earlier had him on shaky ground. He didn't want to send the wrong message, after all.

But as he checked on Elliott before going to his room, Elliott's gaze followed him around and the jitteriness came back. Salvatore motioned, then took Elliott by the hand and led him to the bedroom. He slipped under the covers. Elliott went to the other side, and as soon as he lay down, Salvatore slid over to him.

"I don't think I can stand to be alone right now." He sniffed and then lay still. "I used to think my life was really good. That I had things figured out. Well, at least some things figured anyway. Now I have no idea at all. It's like my life has had the rug pulled out from under it and the things I thought I understood… well, none of them are true." He sighed and Salvatore tugged him a little closer.

"It's like that for everyone now and then. Just hang in there, and we'll all try to figure things out." He really wished he had actual answers of some sort. Instead, he grew quiet rather than offer him useless platitudes that didn't mean a damned thing.

"Is that your version of 'just take it one day at a time'?" Elliott asked, and Salvatore heard the amusement in his voice.

"I guess so." He closed his eyes, and Elliott grew still and quiet. He was like a heater, and yet the last thing Salvatore wanted was to back away from his lithe, trim body. "Just go to sleep. The problems will still be there in the morning, and hopefully when we're fresh, we can look at them from a clearer perspective." At least he hoped so, because right now, they didn't have many answers to all the questions that raced through his mind.

CHAPTER 5

ELLIOTT WOKE and knew that something was different. Roderick had been chasing him on and off for hours, and all he could think of was his stepfather's muscle coming after them. Elliott hated that he thought that way, but the dreams had been so damned real. He hadn't slept very well to start with, but now he sat up and listened. To start with, he was alone, and then a bang from the other side of the house had him jumping out of bed, listening for more. "Salvatore...?" he said, trying not to be too loud. He had no idea what was going on. Elliott cracked the bedroom door open, listening, but the house was quiet, and that unnerved him.

"Elliott," Salvatore said. A door closed at the far side of the house, and Salvatore's footsteps drew closer. "It's okay. I heard something outside and went to take a look. Damned racoons." He yawned and came into the bedroom, then checked out his foot. "Knocked over a shovel." He rolled his eyes.

"Did you break the skin?"

"No. It was just noise. I feel stupid about it, though." He lay back down, and Elliott got into bed as well.

"When I woke up and you weren't here, I didn't know what was going on. I thought someone might have gotten you or something." He shivered, and it wasn't the air-conditioning. His dreams rushed back to him, but they weren't real, and he told himself that over and over as Salvatore held him.

"I'm sorry. You were finally sleeping peacefully, and I didn't want to wake you up. I didn't think it was anyone, but I had to be sure."

"How did you know?"

Salvatore sighed. "Because if someone did actually want to get in the house, I never would have heard one of the trash cans hitting the concrete. They would be stealthy and sneaky as shit. Either that or they'd shoot the place up."

Elliott sighed. "Gee, thanks, that was just what I wanted to hear." He rolled over. "Have you ever thought about a career as a motivational speaker? I think you'd... I don't know... starve." Teasing Salvatore was fun, mainly because he seemed to take it with good grace. Still, it didn't help him feel any better.

"Sorry. I guess I'm used to just telling people what I think." Salvatore held Elliott tighter. "So saying that you should just try to go back to sleep probably sounds pretty hollow."

Elliott lightly smacked him on the arm. "Yeah. You work on that." He smiled, because this was the weirdest conversation and yet he did feel better.

"Okay. I will."

Elliott rolled back over and closed his eyes as Salvatore pressed even closer. "I wish all of this were over." It was easy to say, but things like this didn't just resolve themselves. He didn't move and heard Salvatore's breathing even out as he fell into sleep, but Elliott's mind was on overdrive, and he spent too much time thinking about his stepfather and everything he knew about him. There had to be something, some piece of information that they could use against him. He just needed to figure out what that was.

"Try to sleep," Salvatore said some time later.

"I didn't mean to keep you up," Elliott whispered. He'd tried not to move so he wouldn't disturb him.

"You have to be exhausted, and running over things in your head again and again isn't going to help. It will only keep you up and worrying." Salvatore shifted on the mattress. "Take off your T-shirt and lie on your belly for me." He got out of bed and went to the bathroom.

Elliott pulled off his shirt as he wondered what Salvatore was up to. Then he lay down, closing his eyes, his mind still racing.

When Salvatore returned to the bedroom, he turned on the light on the far side of the room, and it provided just enough glow to see by. Elliott lay still and only turned his head so he could watch Salvatore. He was sexy as hell, bare to the waist, drawing closer. Then he straddled

Elliott's legs, the scent of cinnamon, earthy and soothing, tickled his nose, and slowly, Salvatore ran his hands over Elliott's shoulders.

"God, that's good," Elliott moaned softly. His breathing became deeper as a bubble of calm slowly formed around them. It was almost palpable, with the outside world and all its demands and pressures slowly falling away. It was amazing, but those pressures kept trying to push their way back.

"That's it. Just let go. It takes a few minutes…." Salvatore slowly but firmly stroked down Elliott's back and to the curve of his butt before going upward again, Elliott groaning under the pressure of those amazing hands. "Breathe deep and slow. Let everything go."

"I'm trying." God, that was amazing, and Elliott wanted to just give himself over to him.

"Close your eyes." Salvatore returned to Elliott's shoulders, where he was holding a ton of tension, and slowly worked the muscles, getting them to release and let go. Elliott's arms flopped next to him, and he had no will to move them at all. It took some doing, but his muscles finally relaxed, and Salvatore worked downward, following the tension and getting it out of Elliott's body. "That's a lot better."

Elliott hummed and didn't really say anything. He was finally relaxing toward sleep and slowed his movements.

"I'll do an entire body massage on you some other time. For now, I just want you to be able to rest."

"Yeah…," Elliott breathed. "Think I can do that now."

Salvatore leaned forward and lightly kissed the back of his neck. "Go to sleep, and we can deal with anything else in the morning." He shifted down onto the mattress, and Elliott slowly moved over to give him some room. Elliott closed his eyes, and his mind seemed to have finally settled. He didn't allow anything to puncture the bubble around him, and as Salvatore hugged him close, Elliott felt protected. Finally, after hours of internal turmoil, he fell to sleep.

HE WOKE in the morning to a chime from his phone. He hated that sound, especially at this time of the morning, with Salvatore right next to him. He didn't want to wake up, not for a second, but he forced his eyes open enough to reach for his burner phone and silence the damn thing. He froze at the display. He knew that number, the one from his stepfather's private line in his office. Elliott stared at the number as the phone rang and then grew quiet.

"What is it?" Salvatore asked groggily. "Does Bull need something?"

Elliott shook his head, unable to speak, and showed Salvatore the phone. "It was my stepfather. He managed to get my number." He dropped the phone on the bedding like it was going to scorch him. "What do I do?"

"Nothing." Salvatore sat up, the bedding pooling around his waist. "Don't answer it. Did you set up the voicemail?"

"No," Elliott said.

"Good. He's either trying to unnerve you or is fishing to see if this is the right number. After breakfast we'll get you a new phone and number and dump this one." Salvatore smiled. "Or we can give it to a friend and send your stepfather on a wild goose chase." Elliott liked that prospect. "I have a friend who's going to be leaving for the West Coast in a few days. I'll see if he'll put the phone in his bag and take it with him. The guy is a bit of a conspiracy theorist, so he loves stuff like this." Salvatore chuckled. "He'd do it just to stick it to someone."

"Okay." The last thing Elliott wanted was to touch the phone again. And as if to punctuate that sentiment, it began to ring again.

Salvatore picked it up and powered it down, cutting off the chimes midsequence. "Let's get something to eat, and then I'll call Halston." Salvatore got out of bed, and Elliott couldn't help watching him in only his shorts.

"You know that's not fair."

"What?"

"You walking around like that. It's enough to make a guy want to jump you." Elliott got up as well and walked to where Salvatore stood in front of his dresser. Elliott put his arms around Salvatore's waist, resting his head in the middle of Salvatore's back, inhaling his earthy scent and trying to calm his racing nerves. Salvatore was rock solid and steady, his body hard and unyielding, yet his skin was soft, and Elliott glided his hands over it, taking in the ridges of his belly. "Just when I think I might have some sort of control or idea about what's going on, he manages to turn things on edge." He tightened his grip and took some of the strength from Salvatore. "I hate that. He thinks he can control everything and everyone, reach them no matter where they are." It sucked, and not in a good way at all. "I want him gone." Elliott sighed and closed his eyes, holding Salvatore in the quiet morning.

Salvatore's phone rang, and Elliott tensed, hoping to hell it wasn't his stepfather. Salvatore answered it and spoke quickly before hanging up.

"Is everything okay?" Elliott really didn't want to know. The thought of his stepfather causing more trouble set his teeth on edge, but he was just being jumpy. It couldn't have been him.

"It's fine. That was my mother. She was asking if I was on my way to Philadelphia." Salvatore groaned softly. "I forgot that I had promised her I'd see her today. Sunday is her day off, and...." He sighed. "I'll just call her back and explain."

"No." Elliott didn't want to come between Salvatore and his mom. "You go see her. I'll call...." God, he realized that he didn't have any real friends. "I'll figure something out." Elliott didn't want to move, but life was intervening. "I can hide out at the mall or something for the day. Buy a new phone."

Salvatore sighed and released him. "Get dressed. I'm not leaving you here, and my mother would kill me if I had someone staying with me and she missed a chance to try out some new recipe on them." Salvatore flashed him a smile. "Come on. You take the bathroom first, and I'll get things together while you clean up." He left the room after giving Elliott a lingering look that sent a spike of warmth through him. Elliott went into the bathroom on unsteady legs and closed the door.

He started the water, shaved and brushed his teeth quickly, then took a fast shower. When he returned to the bedroom in a towel, Salvatore was waiting his turn, and it took all Elliott's willpower not to jump the guy. Every time he looked at Salvatore now, heat seared through him and certain parts of his body grew more than a little interested. Still, they were supposed to be in a hurry, so as soon as Salvatore disappeared into the bathroom, Elliott pulled on his clothes, thankful they weren't too tight, and went to the living room, because if he saw Salvatore come out of that bathroom—wet, with his jet-black hair glistening and beads of water sliding over his lightly tanned skin—he was going to fucking lose it and they were never going to make it to Philadelphia.

He also needed a chance to think without the walking, breathing distraction that was Salvatore. Elliott had to get his head where it belonged, and as much as he would love to start things with Salvatore—after all, the guy was a knight in shining armor, and how many of those were there out there? Elliott knew it wasn't many—he couldn't let anyone get sucked into his stepfather's world, and that was already starting to happen. He stared out the window and tried to think of what the hell he needed to do. Elliott wanted to get away from his stepfather, and he knew the only way to do that was to take him down. Nothing short of that would ever get the man to stop.

There was only one way for him to be able to do that. He had to go back into the lion's den, get those papers, and see what the hell he really had. Only then could he plot a way to use them to put his stepfather out of business. But even if he had the smoking gun of evidence against that bastard, it was going to take more than a few papers to bring down Antonio Losquaro.

"What are you thinking?"

Elliott started. He hadn't heard Salvatore at all, he'd been so deep in his thoughts. "About my stepfather."

"No wonder you were clenching your fists," Salvatore told him. "Come on. Let's get out of here for a while." He hugged Elliott from behind.

"Thanks." Elliott wasn't going to argue as he tried to think of his next move.

"Let's go." Salvatore gave him a little squeeze and then checked the locks, and they went out to the garage. Though Salvatore had cautiously made sure the entire house was well locked, Elliott was aware that if his stepfather's men wanted to get inside, a few locks were not going to stop them. But still, it showed Salvatore's care, and Elliott appreciated that.

Once they were in the car, Salvatore started the engine and raised the garage door, backed out, and then closed up the garage before heading down Front Street, taking 83 south to the turnpike, getting on at 43. After passing through the tollbooth, Salvatore put down the convertible top, and they entered the freeway, wind whipping their hair as they raced east.

God, this was exhilarating.

"There are some sunglasses in the glove compartment."

Elliott found a pair and put them on as Salvatore slid his on his face. Elliott sat back, letting the air rush past, clearing out the cobwebs that seemed to have plagued him for weeks now. Salvatore reached across the console and took his hand, squeezing his fingers as he drove.

"What is your mom like?"

Salvatore smiled. "She's a force of nature. In her kitchen she is the absolute ruler. She has the answers and knows what to do, and you don't cross her. There are times when she likes to think that stretches into the rest of the world."

"Like her son?" Elliott snickered.

"Yeah. Mom likes to be in charge. But she's also the first one to praise when things go right, and she rewards initiative and passion."

"She sounds like quite a mom," Elliott said.

"Oh yeah. After Dad died, she picked herself up and figured out how she was going to support the two of us. Mom has more guts than anyone I have ever met." Salvatore squeezed Elliott's fingers. "She's the reason I am the person I am today."

Elliott nodded. "You like your mom."

"Of course I do. Don't you?" Salvatore asked.

"I love my mom, but that's not the same thing. She married the dickhead Antonio because he had money. Yes, she said that she loved him, blah, blah, blah, but I think it's pretty clear that she really loved his money and let that blind her to everything else." Elliott sighed.

"Like I said, I love my mom, but if she wasn't my mom, I don't think that she and I would be friends. That probably sounds dumb, but it's true. She isn't the kind of person I'd want to be like or would want in my life." Elliott hoped what he was saying made sense. "Anyway, it sounds like you would like the kind of person your mom is." He hoped he didn't come across like some weirdo or something.

"I get what you're saying, and yeah… if my mom was someone I met, I think I'd like her. She's pretty cool and she's feisty. I like that she's willing to take charge, make decisions, and then take responsibility for them. She doesn't back down, and she doesn't hide behind someone else." Salvatore seemed proud of her.

They crossed the long bridge over the Susquehanna River and passed the turnoff for the airport. The weather was perfect, sunny and not too warm, an amazing day for a ride in a convertible. Elliott sat back and watched the scenery as it passed outside. There wasn't a great deal other than trees and such, but he took deep breaths and tried not to think too much about the mess with his family.

"Which part of Philadelphia does your mom live in?"

"She's just south and west of downtown, off Rittenhouse Square. She bought the building years ago when no one was moving into the city. I remember her and I working on the house every weekend to fix the walls and repaint. She ripped out the kitchen and then learned how to hang cabinets herself because she couldn't afford to have someone else do it. Man, we must have worked for hours and hours to get them just the way she wanted them. A friend of hers was a plumber, so he helped, and a friend of my dad's did electrical work. She was fussy, but more than willing to put in the work to get what she wanted. Now the house is worth a small fortune and she could sell it and retire if she wanted, but she loves her restaurant and her house. Though she's been talking about making a move to someplace warmer. Don't know if it will ever happen."

"What else does she do?"

"Just about anything she wants. Mom never lets anything slow her down. She told me a few months ago that she had started dating someone. I haven't met him, and I don't know if she's still seeing him or not. Mom is a bit much for a lot of men her age, and they don't stay around for very long. At least they haven't so far."

Elliott chuckled. "Yeah, but does that have anything to do with you?"

"Me?"

"Yeah. I get the idea that not just any guy is going to be good enough for your mom." He put his hand over his mouth. "I can see you intimidating them into running for the door. I mean, come on… one look at you is enough to scare most people, and I suppose you coming in all puffed up was enough to scare away most of the guys who might have been interested in her."

Salvatore scoffed. "I have never done that."

Elliott turned to look at him.

"Not even once." Salvatore winked. "Okay, maybe a few times." He snickered. "Mom is successful, and a few of the guys who wanted to see her were real posers. I never scared away a guy she was actually dating, but a few of them who seemed interested… those I scared the shit out of and they went packing fast." He threw his head back and laughed.

"I see." Elliott smiled. "I think if I could have scared the shit out of Antonio Losquaro, I probably would have."

"I take it you didn't like him."

"I didn't trust him. He came with smiles, and he seemed to enjoy spending his money and time on my mom and by extension me. But I didn't trust him. Mom asked me a few times what it was that Antonio had done wrong, but I could never tell her what. I just knew he was bad, but I didn't have the words then to tell her." Elliott turned away, looking out the side of the car. He wished now that he had somehow found a way to scare him away, that he had done more to keep them apart. But his mom had been so happy, and what was he supposed to do? Make her unhappy? "I should have done more."

"You couldn't have."

"Why? Because I'm small and… not as big as a house?" Elliott demanded.

"No. Because you love your mom and wanted her to be happy. You may not have trusted him, but you couldn't hurt your mom, and regardless of who the guy turned out to be, you did the right thing because it was her choice to make."

"And now the fucker is after me."

Salvatore slowed and pulled off the side of the road, thankfully into the shade. "That was also your choice. You went into his office and copied his papers." Salvatore's gaze bored into him. "I'm not saying that was wrong, but own it. You brought this on, and you did a good thing, but now you're paying the price. So own it."

"Excuse me…?" Elliott didn't get it.

"You did this. Your stepfather is after you because of what you did. You may not have understood the ramifications of it when you made the copies, but you did a good thing. Hold your head up high and look this trouble in the eye." Salvatore clapped Elliott lightly on the leg.

Elliott nodded. Salvatore was right. He had been running on and whining about his evil stepfather, but he needed to take responsibility for his actions and the consequences. Yes, his stepfather was a crook, but he was the one who had put the target on his own back, not anyone else. Elliott nodded slowly as the full realization of what he'd done and the fact that he had to own it weighed on his shoulders. "What do I do?"

"That's what you need to decide," Salvatore said.

"That first day I met you, in the club, the guy who caused trouble called me a little guy… and I felt like one. A scared little bunny who wanted to try to hide and see if the danger would pass me by, and then I could go back to the way things had been." Elliott wiped his eyes from behind the sunglasses with his finger. "But there's no way to go back, and I don't want to be a fucking rabbit."

"That's fully up to you."

"Good." He took a deep breath. "Then when we get back tomorrow, we find a way to take the fight to my stepfather. I need to get those papers, and then we can see what all I've got and figure out the best way to use them. He has to be shitting in his boots, so let's fucking make him really crap himself. There has to be something in there that he can't hide from or just wash away with a few payoffs."

Salvatore checked the rearview mirror and pulled back onto the turnpike. "Now that sounds like something we can work with." He grinned. "And of course, you know his address."

"Yeah."

"So, when we've got the papers, we should send him a package, let him know the kinds of things you have. Let's send him a message." He gripped the wheel tighter. "We could try to tell him that the papers are in safe hands, but if anything at all happens to you, then copies will be sent to every major news outlet, as well as the district attorney at multiple levels. He isn't going to be able to stop that sort of thing. Maybe then he'll back off because it's in his best interest."

Elliott liked that idea, though it wasn't enough as far as he was concerned. His stepfather should have to pay for what he'd done and the people he'd hurt. "But getting him to back off on me isn't enough. It may have been just a couple days ago and maybe a few hours ago, but he's hurting real people. I think I have papers on his bid to buy an apartment building in Pittsburgh. It's a nice one on the edge of downtown, but a little older, and the tenants have leases at rates well below the current market. He wanted to buy the building and take it co-op so he could break the leases and put those people out on the street. Then he could sell the apartments and make a killing."

"I see. That sounds perfectly legal to me. Granted, it's a sucky thing to do…."

"He didn't get the bid, and the building went to someone else. But he was planning some sort of toxic issue in the building, like asbestos. Then he would have to get everyone out and remediate an issue that didn't exist. It would cost him nothing, and then he could sell the units. The bastard. All those people in the building would have their lives uprooted so Antonio Losquaro could make a few more dollars." Elliott sighed. "That's the kind of thing he does. And he doesn't give a damn who he hurts." He tried to remember what he'd copied, but he'd done it in such a hurry, he didn't get a chance to read many of the pages. "You know, I'm tired of talking about him.

It's late Sunday morning and we're on a road trip." He smiled and was determined to let go of this crap, at least for now. "Have you ever brought someone home to meet your mom?"

"Nope," Salvatore asked.

"I see."

"I doubt it. I've moved around a lot, and I never met someone I wanted her to meet. The guys I dated, if you can call it that, weren't the kind of guys that you take home to Mom." Salvatore took Elliott's hand once again.

"And I am?" Elliott asked.

"Honey, you're a cute guy who I really like. My mom is going to love you. So you have nothing to worry about." Salvatore squeezed lightly as they zoomed down the freeway.

The trees along the side of the road began to grow sparse and were replaced with high-rise buildings. Salvatore made the turnoff to the Schuylkill Expressway and they headed toward downtown. Traffic picked up almost immediately and then slowed on and off until they reached the downtown area, and then traffic grew nuts. Elliott sat quietly, letting Salvatore navigate the labyrinth of streets until he pulled to a stop in front of a quaint two-story home.

It wasn't exactly imposing, but was well kept and inviting, with pots filled with flowers in front. Salvatore put the top up, locked the car, and led Elliott up the stairs. They had just reached the door when it opened and a small woman stepped out.

Elliott was shocked, and he turned to Salvatore. She was most definitely Salvatore's mother. She had the same eyes and the same facial features, but she was about two feet shorter and much smaller. For a second Elliott wondered how she could have had a guy as huge as Salvatore.

"I take it you have someone to introduce," she said with a wide smile.

"Mom, this is Elliott."

She took his hand and shook it vigorously. "Call me Josie," she said with so much energy. "How do you know my son? Are you dating, or is this one of those friendship things?"

83

"Mom, you don't get to ask that sort of thing. Elliott and I haven't named what's going on yet. It's new." Salvatore hugged her, and Josie nearly disappeared in his arms.

"Well, how will I understand these things if you don't tell me what's going on?" She backed away and glared up at Salvatore. They hadn't made it inside yet, and Elliott was already wondering what kind of visit this was going to be. He had a feeling that the Spanish Inquisition was going to have nothing at all on Josie. "Maybe if you came to visit more often, I'd know more about my son's life."

"And maybe if you weren't the pushiest woman on the face of the earth, then I could." Salvatore glared back, and Josie grinned after a few seconds.

"Okay. Come on inside, you two. I'll try to be good. But don't expect too much. I'm a mother, after all, and we worry." She motioned inside, and Salvatore let him go first.

Elliott hadn't quite known what to expect, but it certainly wasn't what he walked into. The space was like walking back to the turn of the last century, with the restored woodwork, floors, and lighting that glowed from thick glass shades.

"Josie, this is stunning," he said, snapping his jaws closed. "Salvatore said that you had done a lot of the work yourself. But he never explained how amazing it turned out." He marveled at how warm and beautiful the home was.

"I'm glad you like it." Josie led the way through the living and dining room, which were beautiful and inviting, with comfortable-looking furniture, to the kitchen, which was clearly the heart of this home. "I wasn't sure what to make for lunch…." She lifted down some pans from the rack over the small island and set them on the stove.

"Mom, we came to visit you, not so you could cook for us. This is your day off," Salvatore scolded.

"Though Salvatore has been telling me about your cooking," Elliott said. He sat on one of the stools and looked at mother and son. There was clearly an interesting dynamic between the two of them. They loved each other, that was pretty clear, but there also seemed to be this back-and-forth, push-pull thing going on that Elliott couldn't quite understand.

"Of course I have. Mom is the best." Salvatore grinned and leaned on the island. "But you cook all the time...."

"But not for my wayward son," she argued, and that seemed to tip things in her favor because Salvatore grew quiet, and she got to work. "I have some lovely veal loin, and I thought I could make piccata." She pulled packages and bags from the refrigerator, laying the meat on a board, and got out a mallet to pound the poor cutlets into culinary submission. "I made some of my Caesar dressing."

Salvatore hummed and started helping, tore lettuce, and got everything together. "Mom makes the best Caesar. It isn't traditional, but it has so much flavor... and the garlic." He grinned, and Elliott chuckled.

"I think I'll just stay out of the way." It was cool watching as the two of them worked together.

"Do you and your mom ever cook together?" Josie asked as she breaded the thin veal cutlets and put them into a hot pan.

"No. Mom hasn't cooked very much in years. When she married my stepfather, things changed for her. We moved into a huge house with a staff of three. So someone cooked and someone else cleaned. There was someone to drive the cars. But I know now that he was also my stepfather's body security."

Josie stopped, midactivity. "What kind of family did you come from?"

Elliott sighed. "One where my stepfather needs people around him or he'd probably be dead. He isn't a very good or a particularly nice man. My mom either thinks he's the cat's meow and won't hear anything against him, or is complicit in his activities. We haven't figured that part out yet." At times it felt like the ground under Elliott's feet had turned to quicksand.

"You sweetheart," Josie said, wiping her hands and then patting his. "Children deserve to know where they stand with their parents."

Elliott scoffed without meaning to. "Oh, I understand where things are with my stepfather. He sent someone to bring me home, preferably alive." Elliott didn't want to be grumpy. "Did I mention that he's an asshole?"

Josie turned to Salvatore. "And you're helping Elliott?" She turned the veal as she talked.

"Mom...."

Josie wielded a set of tongs as a weapon, and for a second, Elliott thought she was going to hit Salvatore with them. "But you like him?"

"Yes. Of course I do. I brought Elliott to meet my crazy mother. Duh, I like him. Though I'm starting to think I should bring people I don't like so you could scare them the hell away. And speaking of scaring people away—I hear you're dating someone. Do I need to meet him and make sure he's good enough for you?"

Josie returned to her cooking. "No, you do not. There will be no scaring of Killinger. He's a really nice man and I like him. We've been dating and getting to know each other for two months, and we're planning a culinary tour of the South in January. I'm thinking of closing the restaurant for two weeks, because January sucks for business, and taking some time off. He and I want to sample some good Cajun cooking and a little Southern hospitality."

"Oh, that sounds so good," Elliott said. "I went to New Orleans for a school trip when I was in college. The food was arranged, but Mom told me I had to eat at some local places, and they were the best. The food is simple, with out-of-this-world flavor." Salvatore glared at him as he spoke. "What? I think it sounds like fun."

Salvatore growled. "She's going with some guy... one I haven't met."

Elliott rolled his eyes and patted Salvatore's arm. "What are you? Don't you think your mom knows what's best for her?" Salvatore was acting a little caveman-ish, and Elliott wasn't so sure he liked it.

"You can meet him eventually, but not until I know you aren't going to scare him off. I like Killinger. He's a few years older than me, and he lost his wife two years ago to cancer. He and I are taking it slow."

"Does he have kids?"

"Two girls that I haven't met yet. Killinger and I are still getting to know each other." She seemed a little tentative, and Elliott thought that was probably an unusual situation.

"Okay," Salvatore said. "I won't press it. But I do want to meet him before you go off on a trip together." He walked around to where his mother was cooking. "I need to know that he's good enough for my mother." He hugged her and then moved back.

Somehow that sentiment made her smile. "I think he might be the one." She swallowed and set her attention to cooking.

Salvatore seemed taken aback, though in a good way. "I hope so. You've been alone for a while… too long." He sat next to Elliott once more.

Elliott watched Josie, her movements efficient, not a single one unnecessary. Pasta went into a pot of water, and she went back to the rest of what smelled like the best lunch he'd had in years. Garlic, lemon, capers, a little olive oil, some oregano, all of it mixed, and what came out were three plates that looked as wonderful as they smelled.

"Do you want to eat here?"

"Sure. It's why I designed this island. There's nothing better than eating right where the food is prepared." She took the third stool, sitting on Elliott's right, with Salvatore on his left. "What do you do for a living?"

"I'm a server at the club," Elliott said. "After I left home to get away from my stepfather, Bronco's was the place that was willing to take a chance on me." He took a bite of the veal and moaned softly. The tang of the lemon and creaminess of the butter and herbs was stunning, and he ate some more, suddenly very hungry. "This is amazing."

Salvatore chuckled. "It's my favorite. I always called it veal piccata mundi because eating it is a kind of religious experience." He lightly bumped Elliott's shoulder with his little joke. "Mom was always amazing in the kitchen."

"Did you go to culinary school?" Elliott asked.

"No. I had a passion for food, and after Sally's father died and then I lost my job, I started working in restaurants." She scoffed lightly.

"I was lucky—the first chef I worked for saw something in me. He encouraged me and taught me all he knew. After about six years, he announced that he was retiring and offered me the restaurant. While Sally was in school, I worked all kinds of hours to make the restaurant a success. I paid off the restaurant in four years, and now it's mine. Sort of a home away from home."

"Well, if the food you serve there is anything like this, I can see why." Elliott took some of the salad, and it was stunning as well, bursting with flavor and perfectly balanced with tang, garlic, and a touch of creaminess.

"I use only fresh ingredients, and while I do my own take on a few classics, I serve good, flavorful Italian food." She set down her fork. "In the summer, the fare is lighter, with more vegetables and lighter sauces. In winter, I cook heartier, with more meat and richer sauces that will stick to your ribs on a cold night."

"Mom is amazing." Salvatore finished his pasta and dug into a huge salad.

"Slow down! No one is going to take it from you," Josie said.

"I don't know about that. This is good enough that I may steal some from him," Elliott teased, and Salvatore moved his plate away. Both he and Josie chuckled. Elliott already liked her. "What was he like as a kid?"

Josie put down her fork and rubbed her hands together.

"Mom."

"What? I have been waiting for this for years." She grinned, and Elliott glanced at Salvatore to see if he was really mad. The light in his eyes said he wasn't, not really. "Actually, he was a great son. It was hard on him when he lost his dad. I think he floundered for a few years—we both did." She reached behind him and patted Salvatore on the back. "I think I was most proud of him, and scared for him, when he told me he was going to join the service." Her voice broke a little.

"I bet he was something in his uniform," Elliott said.

"Oh, he was so handsome," Josie said, and Elliott figured he would have used a very different word. The thought of Salvatore in his pressed uniform got his imagination running at full steam. "And he excelled. The flux and confusion of his teenage years was quickly replaced by the confidence and self-assuredness of a man." She grew quiet, and then she turned to Elliott with a twinkle in her eyes. "He used to love watermelon."

"Now come the embarrassing parts?" Elliott asked, and Josie nodded.

"I have a picture of him somewhere eating a slice of watermelon with a diaper halfway to his knees." She chuckled. "I could never get him to stop eating."

"Was his dad big?"

Josie shook her head. "His grandfather. My mom was small like me, but my dad was a big man, and so was his grandfather on his dad's side."

"I was as tall as Mom by the fourth grade." Salvatore finished eating and started taking care of the dishes. "And after Dad died, I was the man of the house. It was my job to help take care of Mom." He seemed happy here. "Though it's not very nice of her to start telling diaper stories."

"I'm sure if you meet my mother, you'll get diaper stories, and 'things kids say' stories, and gosh knows what else." Elliott wasn't sure that was ever going to happen. The last few weeks had completely upended his view of the people he thought of as his family. And now he wasn't sure of very much at all. Was his mother involved with his stepfather's business? It was so easy to think of his mom as innocent and kept in the dark. But she fed him information at the very least. At worst, she was his partner and helped cover up for him. Heck, it was even possible that she knew what his stepfather was doing to try to silence him. Elliott closed his eyes, wishing he had a relationship like Salvatore and Josie had. It was clear they loved each other and even enjoyed each other's company. It had been a long time since he could say that.

"Elliott, honey," Josie said, snapping his attention out of his thoughts. "Are you okay?"

"I'm sorry. Yes." He blinked and forced his mind to the present rather than going over the same things again and again. It was useless and a waste of effort. "Lunch was one of the best I've ever had. Thank you." He took a deep breath and turned to Salvatore, who had cleared the dishes and sat back next to him.

"Would anyone like some coffee?"

"I would," Elliott said.

Josie got up to put some on. She didn't seem to sit still for very long, and while the coffee brewed, she wiped the counters and stove. "What sort of plans did you have while you're here?"

"Well…. Maybe we can go for a walk. It isn't too hot. There are plenty of things to see in the area," Salvatore said as Josie poured mugs and passed them out, along with cream and sugar. Elliott added a little of both to his coffee and sipped slowly. "Do you want to come, Mom?"

"No, thanks. I'm going to spend a few hours with my feet up and watch some television. It's Sunday afternoon and my one full day off. The two of you go on and have fun." She took her coffee to the other room, and Salvatore finished his much more quickly than Elliott did.

"I like it here. Your mom is wonderful," he said softly. She had made him feel welcome within a few minutes. Elliott leaned against Salvatore with a contented sigh and closed his eyes. Salvatore put an arm around his shoulders, and they sat there quietly with Elliott sipping his coffee.

"Mom is great."

Elliott followed Salvatore's gaze, and Elliott snickered. "You want to know more about this guy she's seeing. I can tell." He smiled. "Don't you trust your mom and that she'll know what's best for her?"

Tension instantly rose in Salvatore's body. "It's this guy that I don't trust."

Elliott chuckled. "Maybe, but your mom is the one who likes him and seems serious about him. You aren't the one dating him." He turned. "Unless you have some sort of weird dynamic going on that I need to know about?" God, he loved teasing Salvatore. His face turned red, and he scowled before finally rolling his eyes.

"That's easy for you to say. The guy who keeps wondering if he could have done more to stop his mom from marrying his stepfather."

"Touché," Elliott said. "Still, I couldn't stop her, and neither can you. If you try, it will only hurt your relationship with your mom." He patted Salvatore's hand. "All we can do is let the ones we love make their own decisions." He turned. "You wouldn't want your mom making decisions on who you could date, would you?" Elliott fixed him with a stare and knew he had won the discussion. "Let her be happy. That was what I figured I had to do. Mom always did a lot for me, so I had to do something for her. Granted, if I had known what a piece of crap my stepfather would turn out to be…." He sighed. "Still, it was her decision."

"Yup, and she's the one who will have to live with the consequences, no matter what those are." Salvatore sighed. "I just want her to be happy."

"Then let her be happy and stop worrying about it." Elliott bumped his arm. "Besides, you know what I think?" He drew closer. "I think you like the idea of your mom seeing someone, and all this is you growling just to growl. You think you have to protect your mom, so you're going through the motions when you're really all kinds of happy for her."

"That's what you think, huh?" Salvatore said, running his fingers up his side.

Elliott laughed and squirmed away, but Salvatore held him and tickled some more. "Come on. That's not nice," he protested halfheartedly between laughs. He held on to Salvatore to keep from falling off the stool, while at the same time wanting to get out of range of those tickling fingers. "How do you like it?" Elliott returned fire, but Salvatore just sat there for a second before chuckling.

"I'm not ticklish."

Elliott folded his arms and hit Salvatore with his best grumpy stare. "Now that isn't fair." He finished his coffee, and thankfully Salvatore didn't make him spray his coffee all over the kitchen. When he was done, he brought his mug to the sink. "So what's on the agenda?"

"Let me tell Mom we're heading out. We can walk for a while," Salvatore offered. "I don't think anyone would have followed us to Philadelphia, at least not this quickly."

Elliott nodded as the fun got sucked out of the day. "Why don't we just stay here?"

"We can if you want. Mom is watching a movie or something, and we could go in there and watch it with her." Salvatore caught his gaze. "Like I said, I think it's fine, and I have my phone. We need to get one for you as well, and then I thought we could walk down to the Reading Terminal Market and then farther down Chestnut Street. I can't get tickets because it's too late, but we can walk past Independence Hall. If you want, we can wait in line for the Liberty Bell. I haven't done anything like that in years. They've also unearthed the remains of the President's House used by Washington. They're all close together, and we can stop at the Christ Church Burial Ground and put a penny on Ben Franklin's grave. I know it's really touristy, but it could be fun."

Elliott nodded, reminding himself that he was tired of being scared, ready to duck into his hole at any time. "Okay. Let's go."

Elliott got off the stool, and they said goodbye to Josie before heading out of the house, walking back toward the square and toward downtown, then to the Reading Market.

"I don't remember this."

"When was the last time you were here?" Salvatore asked as they stopped at a corner to wait for a light.

"Oh, I think about ten years ago. It was for a school trip. We were supposed to see the things we talked about today. But the teacher forgot to make some of the reservations, so we never got inside Independence Hall. Mom was pissed as all hell. We were kids, though, so we were fine. We got to see some things, and it was a day away from school." The light changed, and they crossed toward the market.

By the time they got inside, Elliott was warm and thirsty. They got something to drink and wandered the large market building, cooling off and looking things over. Since Josie had fed them so well, there was no need to eat. Instead, they continued on to Chestnut Street and then down to the older portion of the city.

Independence Hall sat at one end of a large green space, with the museum that housed the Liberty Bell across the street. Instead of going inside, they looked at the Bell through the windows and wandered through the park, soaking up the sun.

"I used to come down here all the time when I was a teenager. Me and my friends would play frisbee or football out here. Most of the parks in the city are small, like Rittenhouse Square, but this was big and we could really run and have fun." Salvatore took off, and Elliott followed, passing Salvatore and reaching the far side before he did.

"I won."

"I didn't say we were racing." Salvatore smiled and drew him into his arms.

Elliott glanced around to see if anyone reacted to them, but they seemed to be off on their own. "I get the feeling that with you most things are a competition. I just had to make sure you knew that I wasn't going to let you win… all of the time." Elliott giggled.

"I'm not that competitive."

Elliott rolled his eyes. "I saw you at the gym. You were working out with me, but that guy next to us kept lifting heavier weights, and you had to go ten pounds heavier than him each time, just to show off. I noticed but let you have your fun." He had also cheered internally when the guy gave up and Salvatore continued lifting heavier. "Show-off."

"I see. Then did you notice that he's a jerk and was rude to other people? He hogs the equipment and doesn't let others work in." Salvatore's gaze grew softer. "I had to put the guy in his place. If he wants to run with the big dogs, then he needs to act like an adult and be courteous and play well with others." He shrugged, and Elliott half tuned him out as he leaned against him. It felt nice to be held, and he liked that Salvatore was willing to do it in public. "Let's walk over to the church."

Salvatore released him and led the way down the block and across the street. The graveyard itself was closed, but with Franklin right near the wall and iron grating allowing for access, they both left a penny on the stone.

"If a penny saved is a penny earned, then what is a penny left on Franklin's grave?" Elliott asked.

"Realistically, a penny thrown away?" Salvatore answered. "Or maybe a penny gotten out of your pocket so it doesn't end up on the floor." They looked through the opening into the graveyard. "I took a tour of this place once. Those flat slabs next to the walk, they're underground family vaults with seven or eight graves in them, one on top of the other. The guide told us that they had opened one a few years earlier and it was intact."

"Can you imagine if it wasn't and someone fell through?" Elliott shivered. "Maybe if it were after dark, the vampires would come out." He grinned. "I used to love scary movies as a kid. *Dracula, Frankenstein*—those were cool movies. I was never into the slasher stuff."

"Same here. I liked the gothic stuff. It had a plot behind it and was more than how much blood and guts they could put on the screen." Salvatore stepped back as another group of people approached to give them room. Elliott followed him, and they walked back toward Independence Hall.

"I wonder how many people come here and look for the landmarks in the *National Treasure* movies?" Salvatore asked. "It must drive the guides crazy, or at least I bet it did for a while. It must have died down by now."

Elliott chuckled. "One of the kids in my class had seen the movie at least a dozen times, and he was so mad when we weren't going to get to go inside. He was sure he was going to find some clue to treasure." The building got larger as they drew closer. Elliott looked up toward the bell tower. "I remember being surprised at how small the building actually is. I always thought it would be bigger. But back then it had to be heated by fireplaces...."

"Me too. It's a great building, but I always expected it to be more imposing and stuff. Still, it's pretty cool."

They walked past and back uptown toward Salvatore's mom's. They took their time and went into a few stores along the way.

"Are you interested in soap?" Elliott asked as Salvatore stopped outside a shop window.

Salvatore smiled and crouched down, retying his shoe. "We're being followed," he said softly. "Don't look around. We're going to go into the Walgreens on the next block. It has a second exit, and we'll skip right out. Once we do, just follow me and go as quickly as you can." He straightened up and they continued walking.

"I need something to drink," Salvatore said outside the drugstore and held the door. They went inside and passed through the store. "You go back outside and into the fast-food place right across the street. Stay away from the windows, and I'll be right over." Salvatore turned to the front of the store and stopped at a makeup display.

Elliott continued toward the front and hurried outside, thankful there was no traffic, and went into the Subway. There was a short line of people, and he took a chair away from the windows, watching the doors. He didn't know what the guy following them looked like, but a heart-pounding minute later, Salvatore came in and took him out the front door.

"Where is he?" Elliott asked.

"Probably trying to explain the makeup that I slipped in his pocket after it set off the store alarms." Salvatore chuckled. "Come on. We're going down to the subway. That's the fastest way to get out of here." They went down the stairs, and Salvatore bought tokens. After entering, he led them to one of the trains, with the doors closing just after them. At the next station, they got off and changed trains, then did it again. It was a bit of a whirlwind, and Salvatore kept them moving. "This train will take us to the stop by Mom's."

"But what do we do about your car?"

"I doubt they know why we're here or they wouldn't have followed us. They would have waited until we got back. I'm going to take my car around back and cover it until we're ready to go. Mom has an extra space next to her car. I probably should have done that when we first got here." Salvatore sighed. "But we can hide it in plain sight until we're ready to go home."

Elliott shrugged. "I don't get it. Why follow us here? I mean, it seems like a real stretch for someone to actually follow you and me all the way to Philadelphia. And what is the coincidence that someone might just recognize me all the way on the other side of the state?" He turned to Salvatore as the train pulled to a stop and they got off. "Something else is going on here. I mean, he knows the city I'm living in. My stepfather isn't going to have me followed to the other side of the state. That seems like way too much effort. After all, they know where I work."

They stepped onto the platform, and Salvatore looked around and then led him up the stairs and out of the station. Salvatore turned toward his mother's, and they hurried in that direction. "Go on inside. I'm going to move the car." He climbed in, started the engine, and took off down the street as Elliott knocked softly.

"What are you doing waiting out here?" Josie asked. "Where's Sally?"

"He moved the car around the back. Someone was following us, and…."

She nodded. "He was off on a quest to evade them." She smiled and stepped back so he could go inside. Josie closed and locked the door as Salvatore came in through the back. "Is everything okay?"

"It's fine. I covered the car, so they're going to have to spend some time looking if they want to find it." He went through to peer out the front windows.

"Come on. I'll get us something cold. How about a strawberry-mango margarita? I have this recipe, and it's to die for. Nothing better on a warm day." She started getting things out, and Elliott wondered if he'd fallen down the rabbit hole. They had been chased and Salvatore was on heightened alert, and his mother was mixing drinks like it was a garden party.

"Stay back there and close the door," Salvatore said when the doorbell rang. "It's all right."

Elliott opened the kitchen door and peered around the doorframe. "What's going on?"

"Bull asked me to keep an eye on you," the slight man said as he smiled.

"Is this who was following us?" Elliott asked, and Salvatore nodded. "Has he apologized for the makeup?" Elliott hit Salvatore with a glare.

"Not yet," Salvatore said. "What were you doing? I saw you, and we thought you had been sent by Elliott's stepfather." It was pretty clear that Salvatore was still not completely sold. He pulled out his phone and talked for a few seconds before hanging up, much more at ease. "Sorry about that. But we had no idea."

"Bull had said he was going to let you know, but…."

Just then Salvatore's phone chimed, and he checked it, rolling his eyes. "I just got his texts. Sometimes I hate this thing." He shoved the phone back into his pocket. "Sorry about all this."

"Are you kidding? I had no idea that you had made me, and you took off like a shot. I had to call Bull to find out where you might be in the city in order to catch up with you all." He smiled. "They call me Gem," he said, shaking Salvatore's hand and then Elliott's.

"What did Bull say you were supposed to do?"

"Just watch and make sure you were safe while you were here."

"But how did he know we were coming?"

"Apparently you told him last week that you were planning to visit your mother. So yesterday, he arranged for me to keep an eye on you this morning. I live here in the city, so I was just supposed to make sure you were safe. I didn't mean to cause you any trouble. By the way, no one but me has paid either of you any attention."

"Do you want a drink?" Josie asked as she came in with a pitcher.

"No, thank you. I'm going to be going. I'll keep an eye on the neighborhood to make sure you're safe, and then I'll go on home when you leave." He tipped his imaginary hat and left the house.

"Well, I'll be damned," Elliott said.

"You two have really good friends," Josie said as she poured glasses. "You're both very lucky."

Elliott nodded. "I never had someone in my life like Salvatore or Bull. They've only known me a few days, and they stepped right in to help me." He took the drink. "At first I didn't understand why. Maybe I still don't, but I accepted that they're good people and want to do what's right."

"That's my son," Josie said, motioning to the chairs. "Sit."

Elliott sat. "I guess I'm finding it hard to understand why someone would willingly get involved with the mess I made." *And brought on myself.*

"Oh please. Sally spent years cleaning up other people's messes. But I taught him that you do what's right and you help someone in need." She set down the pitcher and sipped from her margarita glass. Elliott did the same.

"I feel like a fool," Salvatore said as he slumped in the chair. "And you were right. You had this thing with Gem figured out, at least to a degree. It couldn't be your stepfather."

"That's not true. I just didn't think he was going to go to that much trouble. Antonio is many things, but he isn't one to go any further than he has to. The more action he takes, the more he exposes himself to the law and repercussions. So he isn't going to do anything that he doesn't think he can succeed at."

Salvatore nodded at Josie, who leaned forward. "I think you better tell me what's been going on."

Elliott sighed, but it was Salvatore who gave her a brief rundown on what had been happening. "We don't believe Losquaro knows what Elliott has, but we think he's afraid it could be very damaging."

"There's one hell of a lot that you're assuming here, but from what you've said, I think the same thing." Elliott could almost hear the gears whirring quickly in Josie's head. "Young man, you really opened a kettle of fish with this, didn't you? I have to ask what you expected would happen. It sounds as though you knew your stepfather wasn't all sunshine and lollipops."

"I was stupid. I probably should have just left quietly and let him do whatever he wanted. But I didn't know how he'd react, and part of me was tired of him controlling my life, so I guess I wanted some control." Elliott shrugged. He honestly wished he had a clear picture of his own reasons. The more he thought about it, the more simple revenge came to mind. "I guess I was hoping to have some information that I could use as leverage to get what I wanted. I didn't count on him going as far as he has. God, I was just stupid. I put myself and the people around me in danger because I wanted to get influence over my stepfather, and I should have known—no one does that. He won't allow it, and I've seen just how far he'll go to prevent that." Elliott lowered his gaze and set his glass on a coaster on the coffee table. "Maybe I should just give him what I have in return for him leaving me alone."

Salvatore and Josie looked at each other with a kind of silent conversation. Elliott was pretty sure he was missing out on something, but he was damned if he could figure out what it was.

"I think it's probably too late for that," Salvatore said. "Yeah. He may tell you he's going to back off, but he can't let you out of his control now. You've bested him. You got the information, you got away, and you've thwarted his attempts to get you back. You've defied him, and this is a man used to being in control."

"So what do you think his next move is?" Josie asked. "I think it will be big, bold, and scary as hell. Because that's what I'd do if I were him."

"Gee, thanks, Mom," Salvatore said, but Elliott lifted his gaze.

"Go ahead, please." He was doing his best to keep the fear and worry at bay, though it wasn't working very well. "What do you think?"

"He's going to hit something or someone you care about." Her expression became as serious as a heart attack. "If I were to guess, I'd say he's going to use your mother as bait. If he's ruthless, then he'll threaten her somehow."

"But what if she's in on his business?" Salvatore asked.

"Doesn't matter," Josie said as he turned to him. "If he threatens your mom, can you take the chance that he's bluffing?" She cocked her eyebrows. He knew that answer in an instant—of course he couldn't. "Then what do you do?"

"I don't have a choice," Elliott said.

"You always have a choice," Salvatore interjected. "I think we need to get our hands on those papers. Right now, you have them locked away, and you don't really know what you have. If he tries threats, then when we have the papers, we truly have specific information we can use against him. I bet there are plenty of people who would love to see Antonio Losquaro go down."

"Okay. So I get the papers while we try to stay out of his sights." Pittsburgh was a big city, and it wasn't like his stepfather could stake out each and every bank. But Pittsburgh was where his stepfather was the strongest and had the most influence. This wasn't going to be pretty. Elliott drank the frozen concoction down like it was a shot of whiskey. He needed something to fortify his nerves and keep him from shaking to pieces.

"*We*," Salvatore said firmly, and Elliott had never been so grateful for a single word in his life.

CHAPTER 6

AFTER FINDING a place to get Elliott a new phone, Salvatore drove by the house, slowing but not stopping, when they got back to Harrisburg. He continued on instead of heading to the garage.

"What's wrong?" Elliott asked.

"I have a light in the living room that I always leave on. It isn't much, but it's right next to the front window, and it's off." Salvatore silenced the churn in his gut. He hated the idea of someone in his house, but he needed to think straight and keep his own emotions out of it. "We're going on to a hotel." He made a call to Spook through the Bluetooth in the car so Elliott could hear. Salvatore could tell he was freaking out a little.

"Do you want me to go check it out?" Spook asked after Salvatore told him what he suspected.

"I want to say yes, but...." He didn't like the idea of bothering everyone at all hours of the day.

"It's no problem. Jeremy is with some friends for a few days, and I'm sitting here at home. I can run by and take a look." Spook seemed kind of relived to have something to do.

"Thanks," Salvatore said.

"I'll let you know what I find." Spook hung up, and Salvatore felt a little better. Elliott was pale, and Salvatore sighed softly.

"I shouldn't have dragged everyone in this fight. I appreciate everything that everyone is doing, but I hate disrupting all of your lives." Elliott covered his mouth as he coughed. "I hate this shit. I should have left well enough alone."

Salvatore knew how he felt. "Self-pity is so unattractive."

Elliott coughed again. "Thanks. That's good to know."

"What's done is done, and there's no use crying over spilled milk."

Elliott snickered slightly, which was the reaction Salvatore was going for. "Do you think you can use any more platitudes in a single sentence?"

"It's a gift," Salvatore teased as he reached the freeway and then headed across the river. He made a call to a nice hotel he knew and arranged for a room.

"Is the hotel going to be safe?"

Salvatore nodded. "I picked one that only has two floors, and there are plenty of ways out. I also know that this particular hotel has a parking area around the side that's very sheltered, so someone is going to have to specifically look for the car in order to find it, and they are going to have to know this lot exists." It was the most defensible place he could think of at the moment. "I'll request a ground-floor room so we can go out a window as an emergency escape. But I don't think it's going to come to that."

"And tomorrow?"

"You and I get up early in the morning and race to Pittsburgh to get those papers. Then we get back here and figure out our next move." Thank God the club was slow on Mondays and he had that day off. Salvatore would let Bull know their plans so he could be aware. "Your day off is Monday as well, right?"

"Yes." Elliott sat still and didn't say much.

Salvatore missed his talkativeness. He liked the more animated Elliott rather than the quiet and worried version. "Good. Then we'll get up and go." He continued driving and made some extra turns before arriving at the hotel in an industrial park. He'd chosen this hotel because there was a direct freeway entrance at the end of the road and they could be gone. Salvatore parked and they walked around to the front. He checked in and made like he had to get the luggage so the clerk wouldn't think anything was out of the ordinary. Then, once he had the keys, he left and used one of the side entrances and went to the room.

"This is nice," Elliott said as Salvatore came inside and closed and locked the door, while Elliott flopped on the sofa. "I hate feeling like I'm being chased all the time. But I get the idea that one way or another, tomorrow is going to tell the tale." He sighed, and Salvatore watched him eyeing the door.

"Why don't you get a shower and clean up? I'm going to go and see if I can get us something to eat. Then we can go to bed. We need to get up early in the morning. Throw the bolt lock when I leave, and don't open it for anyone but me."

Elliott nodded, and Salvatore grabbed his room key and left. He headed down the hallway to the lobby and out, then jogged to the restaurant they had passed. As jumpy as Elliott was, Salvatore wondered what the odds were that Elliott would be gone by the time he got back with the food.

Salvatore got a few wraps and some salads before returning to the hotel, where he got some cold sodas from the store off the lobby and went down to the room. He tried his key and unlocked the door, then knocked softly. "It's Salvatore."

The swing lock on the side *thunk*ed back, and Elliott opened the door. Salvatore went inside and closed it again, relocking the door behind him. Elliott wore only a hotel robe, his clothes hanging in the bathroom to dry. "I had to rinse them out."

"Of course." Salvatore set the food on the table and started taking things out. "I got chicken salad and roast beef. I like them both, so take whatever you want." He sat down, fatigue taking over. After the driving and the activity, he was tired, yet he was trying to stay awake so he could keep whatever wolves might be circling at bay.

"Thanks." Elliott seemed just as rolled thin as he was, and they ate quietly. Salvatore was too tired for conversation, and thankfully Elliott didn't seem to want to talk either. The silence didn't seem oppressive, and that surprised him a little. It was also nice to know that neither of them felt the need to fill the still times with chatter. Salvatore ate his roast beef and then some of the salad, leaving the rest for Elliott. He was full and left the small living area to lie down on the bed.

He turned on the television and sat propped up on pillows, toeing off his shoes. After a little while, papers crunched in the other area, and Elliott came in and sat on the other side of the bed. Salvatore sighed and tried not to let his attention waver to Elliott in his robe and what might just be under there if he were to tug at that cord around his waist. He'd promised that he was going to take things slow. Hell, Elliott had been ready to go, and *he* had been the one to put on the brakes. Now Salvatore couldn't keep his mind off Elliott, and each time he shifted, Salvatore wanted to slip closer. He knew what Elliott felt like in his arms, and now he wanted to know more, like what his naked skin felt like against him and how hot Elliott would get when they made love. Salvatore imagined Elliott as a quiet but intense lover who used his hands and lips to communicate what he wanted.

Crossing his legs so things didn't become too obvious, Salvatore forced himself to watch the old movie on the TV rather than let his mind wander over and under Elliott and that damned white robe. "Is this okay? You can watch something else if you like." He handed Elliott the remote, and Elliott found one of those cooking shows.

"I love watching these. They always make me hungry, though sometimes the food looks like something I wouldn't feed a dog." He chuckled, and it was good to hear Elliott laugh.

"I love your smile," Salvatore said with one of his own, then closed his eyes, trying not to dwell on how close Elliott was or how his scent, light with a hint of sweet, tickled his nose. He got off the bed, went to the bathroom, and used the shower and the second robe. At least he felt clean when he came out.

Elliott was already under the covers, and he blinked up at Salvatore like he wasn't sure what was next or what to expect. Salvatore had no intention of jumping the guy, but he looked so adorable and kind of vulnerable like that.

Salvatore's phone chimed, and he breathed a soft sigh at his reprieve, turning away from Elliott and taking the chance to clear his head. He picked it up and answered Spook's call. "Was someone there?"

"I think so at one point. I'm not sure when they left, but they didn't leave much of a trace behind. Whoever it was didn't seem to touch anything, and I expect they think they were clever enough that you wouldn't know they were there. The doors had been locked and nothing was touched, but they forgot one thing. Whoever was here wore an expensive French cologne, and the scent hung in the air after them. Fragonard makes good product, but it tends to be strong and it lingers for a long time."

"Thank you."

"I left as well and came back home. I'm thinking that tomorrow evening, our stalker should get a reception he isn't expecting. I'll call you in the morning, and we can figure out a little surprise for him." Spook seemed kind of happy, like this was really his thing.

"We appreciate the help." Salvatore ended the call, put his phone on the nightstand, and explained about the call to Elliott. He turned out the lights, leaving on the television, and climbed into bed, putting the robe on the chair. The sheets were crisp and soft, easily sliding against him.

"Sally," Elliott said, and Salvatore growled at the name only his mother used. And it was going to stay that way.

"You can call me Sal if you have to, but not that." He rolled on his side. "El." He smiled and reached to Elliott's smooth face, stroking his cheeks. "You are beautiful." In truth, there was a part of him that was afraid he was going to hurt Elliott.

"And you're as big as a house. It's a good thing I have this kink for big guys." Elliott slid closer. "I know what you said the other night, but I'm also starting to think that if I sit back and wait for you, it'll be until hell freezes over." He slid next to him, then brought their lips together. Elliott kissed him, need and intensity growing by the second. Salvatore wound his arms around him, and Elliott pressed closer, pushing him onto his back and climbing on top of him. Damn, Elliott was like a live wire, thrumming with energy. Salvatore stroked down his back, cupping his small, tight butt, and Elliott vibrated on top of him.

"Jesus…." Salvatore groaned when Elliott backed away, their gazes meeting. "I wasn't expecting this."

"What?" Elliott asked him. "Did you think I was some kind of shrinking violet?"

Salvatore nodded. "At least a little more tentative."

Elliott chuckled and shrugged. "If I'm going to do something like this, I figure I should go all the way. And somehow I don't think you're the kind of man who wants to be with a guy who's all demure. You're a big guy with a lot of power, and I want to feel it."

Salvatore shivered because he wanted that so badly. He opened his mouth to say that he'd be careful, but Elliott kissed him, taking possession of his mouth. God, this was exciting, and he held Elliott closer. Damn—he was so much bigger than him, and Salvatore really was afraid that he'd hurt him, but Elliott was fearless. And for the first time since he'd met him, it seemed that Elliott was the one in charge. Initially the thought sort of startled him.

"Is this too much for you?" Elliott asked. "I can tone it down and...."

Salvatore kissed Elliott hard. "You be yourself in bed and out of it. I don't want you changing who you are—any part of what you want—because of me." He smiled and nipped at Elliott's lower lip.

"But I take it you're the one used to being in charge, and I never gave any thought to how you might like things." Elliott paused. "I guess before we got this far, we should have talked about things like top and bottom." He cocked his eyebrows, and Salvatore swallowed hard. He had to admit he had never given that sort of thing much thought. Salvatore was a big guy, and the men he met all just assumed that he would be the one doing the driving.

"Okay...." He cradled Elliott's cheeks in his hands. "What do you want?" He lowered his voice and brought his lips closer to Elliott's ear. "What is it that fuels your wildest fantasies? Is it sliding your cock into me? Or is it you being on top, riding me until your eyes roll back in your head?" Elliott shivered, and Salvatore smiled. He was getting a pretty good idea of what it was that Elliott liked.

"Maybe...." Elliott bit his lower lip. "A guy shouldn't give away all his secrets. If you have to find things out for yourself, it makes things so much more interesting."

Salvatore chuckled. "So you want me to play explorer." He stared into Elliott's midnight blue eyes. Damn, he loved how they seemed to darken when Elliott was turned on. Salvatore shifted his hands and then cautiously manhandled Elliott down onto the mattress, not breaking his gaze, his hands slowly roaming over Elliott's skin. His thumbs found his pert nipples, making slow circles around them, plucking occasionally, Elliott's breath hitching.

"Sal…." He quivered, and Salvatore did it again just to hear Elliott gasp. That sound was worth just about anything. "That's so good."

Salvatore hummed softly, sliding lower down the bed, his hands remaining busy, his tongue blazing a trail down Elliott's belly, kissing his soft, slightly salty skin. He loved the way he tasted and was ready for more. Flicking his nipples, Salvatore closed his lips around Elliott's slender cock, sucking him deeper to a chorus of soft, breathy groans that seemed to fill the room, building one on top of the other. He took more of him, relaxing his throat until he had all of him, tongue tasting him even further.

"Oh God…," Elliott gasped, his leg shaking against the bedding.

Salvatore loved the feel of a cock sliding over his tongue, and Elliott tasted like heaven. He adored the little sounds Elliott made even more, each one encouraging him forward until Elliott's breathing became more ragged and he gripped the bedding, eyes clamping shut. That's when he backed off.

"Damn…," Elliott groaned. "I…."

Salvatore grinned. "I know. But I want you to last." He brought his lips to Elliott's, letting him taste some of himself.

"But I don't think I can take that again…." Elliott sighed, and Salvatore held him, rolling them over until Elliott was on top once more. "You know I'm not going to break."

"Yeah, but…." Salvatore held Elliott closer, roaming his hands over Elliott's buttcheeks, sliding his fingers between them, eliciting the most amazing little vibrations from him. "Is this what you like? Or do you want me?" Salvatore didn't bottom often. It wasn't what most guys thought when they saw him, so he took the top role.

Elliott lifted his head away. "Are you serious?" He blinked rapidly, as though he needed to make sure he had heard properly.

"Of course I am. I want you to be happy," Salvatore whispered. "And I want you to know that between us, when the bedroom door is closed, we can be and do whatever we want."

Elliott actually sighed and smiled. "I think I'd like that…. Maybe next time."

"Okay…." Salvatore was a little confused. "What do you want now?"

"That 'me on top, riding you' thing." Elliott grinned. "Have you got stuff?" Of course, neither of them had anything at all. It wasn't like they had planned on staying at a hotel. He snickered and rolled his eyes. "Then I guess we'll just have to make do with other things." Elliott shimmied away and straddled his legs, wrapped his fingers around Salvatore's cock, and stroked slowly.

"Yeah…?" He swallowed hard as Elliott seemed to touch him just the right way. His hips came up off the bed, willing for more, but Elliott continued his slow pace, driving Salvatore out of his mind. "I'm not going to break," he said, using one of Elliott's lines.

"Oh, I know that. I want you to remember this for a long time." Elliott leaned forward to kiss him, and then when he pulled away, licked a trail down Salvatore's chest and belly, coming close to his cock but never taking him.

Salvatore crossed his eyes and held on to the damn bedding. He knew he'd started this, but Elliott was a master of the art of anticipation, and he could only beg quietly, knowing his pleas were most likely to fall on deaf ears, at least for now. "And here I thought you were more innocent than this."

Elliott backed away, and damned if his cheeks didn't pink up. "Well, I don't have a lot of actual experience. I mean, I haven't had sex with a bunch of guys or anything, but there are ways that you can learn about things like this." The color rose even more.

"I see. So what kind of instruction were you watching?" Salvatore breathed deeply and cleared his muddled head.

Elliott shrugged. "You know…." God, it was cute how he could be so forceful at times and shy at others. Not that Salvatore wasn't that way as well. There were some things that were so easy to talk about, but when it came to sex, there were things that were private, and opening up was just hard.

"Do you watch a lot of porn?"

Elliott shook his head. "But I did sometimes. I lived at home with my mom and stepdad, who I now know kept closer tabs on me than I realized. So sometimes…."

Salvatore chuckled and drew Elliott up to him. "It's hot thinking of you alone in your room, pleasuring yourself. Was it to images of big, muscular guys?"

Elliott shrugged. "There was one who really turned me on. He had a big chest like you, and a furry belly, but you're way hotter." Elliott nuzzled close. "You're real, and he was just some image. Also, you're just a lot sexier than him." He smiled a slightly crooked smile.

"That's a relief," Salvatore said, and placed Elliott's hands on the headboard. Then he slid down under him until his lips slipped around Elliott's cock. Salvatore gripped Elliott's butt, controlling his movement as he took him deep, to Elliott's sharp gasp for breath, and then a slow moan filled the whole room once again. He was quickly falling in love with those noises, and he wanted Elliott to remember this night forever.

"Sal," Elliott whimpered, his legs shaking a little. Salvatore didn't let up, holding Elliott and taking him to the brink, backing away, and then doing it again. When he thought Elliott was about ready to explode into pieces, he sucked him hard and held him as Elliott stiffened and tipped over the edge, swallowing Elliott's release. He let him down gently, hugging him tightly as Elliott settled on the bed in a bubble of warmth. Salvatore listened to him breathe and rubbed his belly gently, letting him enjoy the postcoital haze. As far as he was concerned, those few minutes were some of the grandest in existence. Everything was quiet and the world didn't exist for just that small period of time. It was the time for the two of them.

Elliott rolled over eventually, and Salvatore lay facing him, their lips a few inches apart. "What about you?"

It seemed like Elliott could hardly move and was relaxed, which was what he wanted. "Go to sleep," Salvatore whispered, and Elliott hummed and closed his eyes. There was plenty that could wait until tomorrow, and Salvatore figured they were going to need all the rest they could get.

CHAPTER 7

"JUST BE careful," Bull was saying through the car Bluetooth as they zipped down the Pennsylvania Turnpike. Before they left, Spook had shown up at the hotel with clothes and things from Salvatore's house, so at least they had been able to change clothes.

"We will," Salvatore said. "I know we're going into the lion's den."

"Yes, and unfortunately I don't have any support that I can offer you. That area of the state is surprisingly devoid of the people I served with over the years."

Elliott suppressed a sigh and tried to ignore the stab to his gut.

"Watch closely, get what you need, and get the hell out."

"We will. The plan is to go to the bank, get the papers, and get out of town."

"It's not like I'm going to drop in at my stepfather's to say hello," Elliott said. He had to remind the two of them that he was in the car.

"No. But your stepfather has a huge network of contacts and people. So I want you to remember that as soon as you make yourself known at the bank, it's likely a ticking clock."

"Why?" Elliott asked. "Banking is confidential."

"It's supposed to be," Bull said. "But if your stepfather has a contact at the bank or in the organization, all it takes is someone to tip him off that an account with your name on it has been referenced. Then it's a matter of how fast your stepfather can mobilize to intercept you. I'm not saying that will happen, but that's how you have to think. So, don't loiter, and get the hell out of there and back to where we can control the situation."

Elliott nodded. "I think I understand. His power is centered there."

"Yes. Just be cautious and be aware of everything that's happening around you."

"We will," Salvatore agreed. "We'll call you as soon as we're on our way out, and we can figure out a plan of attack based upon what we have." They said goodbye, and Bull ended the call.

Elliott tried like hell not to be nervous.

"Bull is right. There isn't much that he isn't going to know, and with him looking for me, he's going to have feelers out everywhere." He sighed and put his hand over his chest where one of the keys to the deposit box hung around his neck under his shirt. "Unfortunately, the bank isn't particularly close to the freeways. It's downtown. I thought I could get lost down there, but that means it's going to be harder for us to get in and out of town." He cursed under his breath that he hadn't thought further ahead. All he had wanted to do was get the papers safe and then disappear, and he'd figured a crowd was the best way to do that. He bit his lower lip.

"That's all right. Downtown means lots of turns and ways to evade being followed. I know there's plenty of traffic, but we can get in and out as fast as possible." Salvatore turned to him. "Was there something else? I get the feeling there's more. Something that's missing."

Elliott nodded. "It's so stupid. I have a real close friend. He hates the bastard as much as I do. And when I had to leave, he said he'd take care of Buster for me." Elliott clenched his fist. "My apartment in Harrisburg doesn't allow dogs, just like I thought, and since I had to leave in a hurry, Traynor promised to look after Buster." He refused to cry. It had been the right thing for Buster, even if it had nearly broken his heart.

"You have a dog," Salvatore said, and Elliott nodded. "You never mentioned that before."

Elliott shrugged. "I couldn't talk about it. Buster is better away from me and from the house. He loves Traynor and is probably happier. He has a yard and a place where he can run and go outside. I couldn't give him that with my situation." He turned away and wiped his eyes, refusing to cry, dammit. "I just want to try to see him." That would be enough. "But we all can't have what we want, and getting the papers is way more important."

Salvatore gripped the wheel tightly. "So you're telling me that you left everything, including your dog, in order to get the hell away?"

"I had to. I knew that without all that much money, I couldn't get a place where I could live with him."

"But you never said anything." Salvatore's voice broke a little. "You should have told me." Not that that would have done anyone any good, and no one would have been able to change it.

"What was I supposed to do? Talk about it so I could blubber all over the place like some stupid baby?" He took a deep breath to try to push the immense loss down deeper, but it didn't go away, only becoming more urgent. "Maybe we can see him before we go to the bank. Traynor should be home. He's a nurse and works nights, and we don't have to stay long." He was prepared for Salvatore to say no, but he nodded instead, and Elliott closed his eyes, sitting back, the ache in his heart easing a little.

Salvatore didn't say anything for quite a while, the tires humming as they rode, giving Elliott plenty of time to think. "I don't understand why you didn't say anything."

"Because I guess it didn't matter. He's with Traynor and he's happy and has a place to run. I can't provide that in Harrisburg." He shrugged. "I do miss him, though."

"What kind of dog is he?" Salvatore asked, half grinning. "I don't know why I think of him as this little yippy toy poodle with big expressive eyes, running around your feet in circles, happy to see you." He laughed, and Elliott scowled at him.

"You're part right. Buster is a labradoodle, but about fifty pounds or so. He has the energy and the bright eyes, but he isn't yippy. He loves to take walks and go outside. He's leash-trained, and I took him to obedience and obstacle course classes. He's really smart."

"How long has your friend had him?" Salvatore asked.

"About two months now. Buster and Traynor love each other, and Traynor has said that he will adopt Buster if that's what I want. But I can't give him up permanently, not yet, even though it's probably the best thing. The bastard started threatening Buster, so Traynor said he'd take him until I could figure something out."

Salvatore nodded. "Did you think that your stepfather might use Buster against you?"

Elliott gasped. "No. He hates Buster and was always complaining about him shedding or something, which he doesn't do. Buster has curly poodle-type hair and has to be trimmed every six weeks or so. It's that awful Doberman that the bastard has that sheds all over everywhere and pees anywhere in the house she wants, except in my stepfather's office. That dog is one manipulative bitch." Elliott put his hand over his mouth, giggling a little. "She would pee on the carpet and leave the room so Buster would get blamed for it. After Buster was gone, he complained that Buster taught his stupid dog to go inside." Elliott rolled his eyes. "The man is nuts most of the time, and nothing is ever his fault, including the fact that he never trained his dog to be anything but mean to everyone."

"I see. Were you afraid of his dog?" Salvatore asked just before they passed into one of the tunnels. "I hate these things. When driving, I'm always looking for a way out in case of danger or a threat, and there never is one in these." He sped up as much as the car in front of them would allow until they burst out into daylight once more.

"Bessie? No. I used to sneak her food all the time when he wasn't looking. That dog loves me. She didn't like Buster because they both wanted to be alpha dog and she lost when Buster beat the crap out of her more than once. But I figured that the easiest way to drive the bastard crazy was to take away one of his methods of intimidation." Elliott sighed and thought about Buster. Maybe it wasn't a good idea to go see him. Elliott still didn't have a place for him, and leaving him again was going to be damned hard. It was probably best if he let Traynor adopt him. At least Buster would have a good forever home.

"Let's visit Buster. That way you can see him. Do you think your stepfather might be watching your friends? He could see if you contact them, or does he even know where your dog is?"

Elliott sighed. "I don't know. He and Traynor never liked each other. Traynor thought Antonio was a jerk, and he's my friend... I mean...." He knew he wasn't making much sense. "I doubt he'd be watching him. Antonio was happy that Buster was gone, and when he asked where he was, I said I had given him to a friend. He seemed happy and mumbled that he was glad the rug pee-er was gone." Elliott wanted to strangle him again. It was an emotion he seemed to be having a lot lately. "I didn't realize how stifling things had been at home until I managed to get out."

"Abusive, controlling relationships sneak up on us. They don't usually start out that way, but they grow into them slowly. There are plenty of people, men as well as women, who wake up one day and wonder how things got so bad... or how they can get out when they are so trapped and afraid."

"I wonder if things are like that for my mom sometimes. I think she has to see the kind of guy he is, and yet she goes forward happy and seemingly content no matter what anyone says." Elliott sniffed as a wave of sadness coupled with frustration washed over him. "I tried to tell her, and she said that I had to be making things up."

"Gaslighting," Salvatore said. "It could be that simple."

Elliott nodded. "Yeah, I guess so." He liked to think of his mom as the woman he knew before she married Antonio. He thought that they had been happy enough. Even if the two of them hadn't had many material things, they'd had each other. Then she'd met and married Antonio, and the things his money could buy seemed more important than the life and care they had before. Elliott knew his mother loved him, but he honestly thought she loved her easy, well-ordered, money-is-no-object life even more. "I don't know." And that was the part that hurt the most. He wasn't sure if he could trust his own mother at all when it came to Antonio.

They passed Somerset, and a half hour later approached the turnpike exits at the outskirts of the city. Elliott gave Salvatore directions to Traynor's house, and pretty soon they pulled up in front of a ranch home that had been built in the fifties. Traynor had done a lot to update the exterior of the home. As soon as they pulled to a stop in the driveway, Elliott got out. Near-frantic barking come from inside, with Buster peering out the front window.

Traynor met them at the front door, looking a little groggy, but he pulled Elliott into a hug just as soon as he got close enough. "God, it's good to see you. I was getting worried because I haven't heard from you in so long." Traynor released him, and his eyes widened as he seemed to see Salvatore for the first time. "Who is the walking wet dream? I just woke up, and man, am I still dreaming? If I am, I want to go back to bed… with him," he whispered dramatically.

"Salvatore, this is my friend Traynor." They shook hands. "Salvatore is helping me out with some of the shit with the asshole stepfather. Have you seen him or any of his minions?"

"Gosh, no." Traynor opened the door, and Buster raced out, jumping to get Elliott's attention. He leaned down, petting, stroking, and getting kisses as Buster practically bent himself into a half moon to get as much attention as he possibly could. "That ass knows to stay away. I saw him at the hospital last week and asked if he was there to get the hemorrhoids removed from his brain." Traynor laughed as he opened the door once again. "Come on inside. I can get you something to drink."

Elliott nodded and continued petting Buster as they went inside, and Traynor closed the front door. Elliott sat down on the sofa, and Buster jumped on his lap, his tail going a mile a minute as Elliott buried his face in Buster's neck, holding him and petting slowly. He needed this so badly. "What was the bastard at the hospital for?"

"Tests of some sort. He wasn't in my wing or I would have taken a look at his records the first chance I got. I hope it's some dick-eating disease and the damned thing falls off. Of course, since the guy is a dick, he would just disappear and put all of us out of his misery." Traynor seemed pleased with his witticism and turned to Salvatore. "What can I get you, tall, dark, and too sexy for words?"

Elliott growled, and Buster stopped his wriggling to look up at him as Salvatore slowly sat next to him.

"Okay, I get it. He's spoken for. Dang it." Traynor smiled. "What would you like to drink?" he asked, this time much more like Salvatore was a human being rather than a piece of meat. "Don't mind me. Sometimes I get too swishy for even my own good."

Elliott answered and continued petting his dog, and Salvatore checked out the window a few times until Traynor returned with some sodas.

"Are you here to take Buster?" Traynor asked. "He goes to the door all the time to check for you. You know he's welcome to stay here and I'll adopt him if that's what you want, but…."

Buster had settled in his lap, and Elliott continued petting him. He didn't dare look at Salvatore. "I don't think I can take him, at least not yet. Stuff with my dickhead stepfather is a mess right now." He hadn't told Traynor about the papers and things. He'd only said that he had to get out of town and that he couldn't take Buster with him. Elliott thought he'd be safer if he didn't know anything.

"I figured with the way you left town so quickly that it had to have something to do with him." Traynor popped open his soda, and Salvatore gently stroked Buster's head.

"We can't stay very long," Salvatore reminded him.

"Why not?" Traynor asked. "Are you guys on the run or something? I tried calling but never got an answer." He was always pretty dramatic, only this time he was close to the mark.

"Not exactly, but Antonio has been after me and we need to get some things and get out of town as quickly as possible." Elliott buried his face in Buster's fur, wondering how in the hell he was going to be able to leave him again. "I had to get a new phone and everything." He showed it to Traynor and then texted him. "Don't give the number to anyone."

"It's all right. If Traynor can get Buster's things together quickly, we'll take him with us. Buster can stay at my house until after this is over, and then you can figure out a better place for the two of you to live."

Elliott smiled and nodded through a stab of disappointment. He should have known that getting too close and too comfortable with Salvatore was probably not a good idea. Granted, they hadn't known each other but a week or so, but Elliott had become comfortable enough with him so quickly. God, his head was really messed up right now. But still, he hoped after last night that things with Salvatore were becoming serious and that Salvatore cared for him. Something about finding a place to live on his own with Buster left him cold, like some of the warmth had been pulled out of the room all of a sudden.

"Are you sure?" Elliott asked.

Salvatore leaned closer. "Yes. We'll figure things out, but it's pretty clear that you miss Buster and that he misses you."

"Let me get his things together." Traynor jumped to his feet, and Elliott sighed. This was so tempting and it was what he wanted, no doubt about that. But was it the right thing for Buster? What if his stepfather hurt him or something? God, he wanted Buster with him so badly.

"Are you sure we should do this?" Elliott lifted his gaze.

"Sweetheart, I'm not sure of anything except the fact that I know your heart will break if you have to leave him behind." Salvatore bit his lower lip slightly, like he was nervous. That set Elliott's belly fluttering because Salvatore was usually so confident. "Though I don't know where we'll be staying tonight. Spook was going to see if he couldn't deal with our visitor from last night. But we may end up at a hotel. I know it isn't ideal for this guy, but we'll make it work."

Elliott hugged him and closed his eyes, just letting himself be content, if only for a few seconds.

Traynor returned with two cloth shopping bags of things. "Are you sure you don't want to stay for a little while?"

Salvatore took the bags. "No. Thank you."

Buster jumped down, then nosed the bags. Elliott stood and hugged Traynor. "Thank you for taking care of him. I appreciate it so much."

"I loved having him, and it's going to be lonely around here now. Maybe I'll have to get a dog of my own." Traynor knelt down and gave Buster some goodbye scratches, and then Elliott and Salvatore, with Buster right behind, went out to the car.

Buster jumped right in and into the back, head looking out between the front seats. Salvatore put the things in the trunk, and then they got in the car. Elliott waved as they backed out of the drive and took off down the road, making a few turns out of the subdivision and out to the main road, where Salvatore pulled into a grocery store.

"What do we need from here?" Elliott asked as Salvatore got out.

"Take off Buster's collar for me," he asked, then left the engine running and closed the door. Salvatore opened the trunk, and Elliott removed the collar and handed it to Salvatore through the open window. It was the same one that Buster had had when Traynor first took him.

After about five minutes, Salvatore returned and placed a small device in his hand. It looked about the size of a watch battery. "What's this?" Elliott lifted his gaze as the idea dawned on him. "No way. You mean Traynor…?"

Salvatore nodded. "It's possible, or the dog collar could have been bugged long ago. But it seems unlikely."

"But why? He hates Antonio." Elliott felt as though his heart was going to stop.

"I don't know. Maybe someone offered him money to do it. Convinced him that they needed to know where you were to help protect you. I don't know." Salvatore checked the collar and handed it back. Then he put the car in gear and slowly made a circuit of the lot. A truck was pulling out, and Salvatore took the device and tossed it into the bed of the truck. At the exit, the truck turned left, and they turned right, hopefully sending whoever had been after them on a wild goose chase.

Elliott sat stunned in the front seat, stroking Buster and wondering how he could have been so wrong about his friend. He wanted to cry as yet another part of his life was ripped away. Who else had his stepfather turned against him? "Let's get those papers and get the hell out of here." It was clear that there was less and less for him here.

CHAPTER 8

SALVATORE'S HEART pounded. He almost hadn't told Elliott about his friend. It had hurt him to do so, but Elliott needed to know. "When this is over, talk to him, find out what happened." Salvatore knew there was the possibility that Elliott's stepfather already knew they were in town. Traynor could easily have called him, and that only added to Salvatore's anxiety and urgency.

"I don't know if I can ever have anything to do with him," Elliott said, crossing his arms over his chest.

"That's your choice." Salvatore pulled up to a light. "Where do we need to go to get to the bank?"

Elliott brought up the GPS and entered the information. "This can give you basic directions from here. It's on the other side of town, and we should probably take the freeway there and after that...." Elliott swallowed hard. "I don't know what's going to happen." His hands were shaking by the time he was done, and they were moving forward once again.

Salvatore wasn't familiar with Pittsburgh, and he followed the disembodied GPS voice to the bank and pulled into a parking space, ensuring they had a way to make a quick exit if necessary. "You go in and get what you need. I'm going to stay out here with Buster and keep watch. Don't let them stall, and when you get the papers, hurry out as quickly as you can. We can't waste any time."

"I remember what Bull and Spook said." Elliott got out, hurried to the door of the bank, and went inside.

"I know," Salvatore said when Buster whined. "I miss him too." He patted the dog's curly-haired head, and Buster leaned a little closer to him before jumping between the seats and onto the passenger seat.

Salvatore scanned the parking area, grateful that no one seemed to be coming and going at the moment. Still, as time passed, he found himself checking out every car that went past on the street. He'd kept the engine running for the air-conditioning, as well as so they could get away quicker, if necessary. Salvatore kept watch, growing more and more anxious. He stared at the clock and then the entrances to the bank parking lot.

Finally he saw Elliott through the glass door. He was shaking hands with someone and then came out. Salvatore drove over, and just as Elliott tugged open the door, a large black SUV rolled into the lot on the far side. Salvatore waited until Elliott closed the door and then pulled out into traffic, barreling just in front of a blue Toyota that blew its horn at him. Not that he cared in the least. They needed to get away.

"Hang on, we're being followed, and I'm going to need to lose them before we get onto the highway."

"Buster, sit down," Elliott said.

Salvatore hoped the command was successful because he made the next right turn and then another, followed by a left onto a one-way street going the direction he needed. The GPS voice was going a little crazy as she kept telling him to proceed to the highlighted route, even as he made another turn and headed out toward the highway.

"Are they gone?"

"No. There's another car that's trying to come up on us." He sped up and zipped through a light, then made another turn as the other car got caught. There was the possibility that he was being paranoid, but Salvatore wasn't taking any chances. He continued out toward the highway. Then he entered highway traffic and headed back toward the turnpike. He thought of going the other way and trying to throw them off, but the people who had both his and Elliott's back were in Harrisburg, so his goal was to get to them as quickly as possible. "We lost them this time, but it's pretty clear that they know where we're heading." Salvatore sped up as much as he dared. "What sort of things do you have?"

Elliott opened the folder on his lap and began going through the sheaves of papers. "I know I have a number of shipping invoices and manifests. There are also legal documents and bank records."

He continued going through them. "There are a number of invoices and…." Elliott paused midsentence. "Oh my God."

"What?" Salvatore didn't take his eyes off the road.

"Planning documents for a deal that seems to be in the works. I bet the city would love to get their hands on these." Elliott grinned. "I don't see anything blatantly illegal in any of this. I mean, there may be shady things, but then again…." He put the pages together.

"I bet Harry at the club can figure out what's there."

Elliott nodded. "I hope so. I'd hate to have done all this and put you and everyone in danger for my stepfather's laundry list and grocery bills." He put the papers in the folder and closed it. "I was hoping for something… I don't know."

Salvatore patted Elliott's leg. "He wasn't going to write down his entire nefarious plan like a supervillain for you to find. There are pieces of the picture in there, and what we need to do is find them. But what you have must scare him enough to want to come after you. Either that or there are things in his office that he thinks you might have copied, and that's what has him freaking out." He sure as hell hoped there was something in those papers, if for no other reason than to give Elliott some bargaining power one way or another. If they had nothing, then it was going to require that they run one hell of a bluff in order to get Losquaro to back off.

"Should we call Bull and let him know that we have the papers?" Elliott asked, and Salvatore made the call.

"You're both okay?" Bull asked as soon as he answered the phone.

"We had a little trouble, Elliott got the papers, and we're on our way back. I expect some sort of welcoming committee when we get there, though. As we suspected, they were waiting for some sort of activity, and we had to make a stop and found out that his stepfather has been busy." Things were going to get ugly. If Elliott's stepfather was willing to take the chance of trying to corrupt some of Elliott's friends, then he was going to stop at nothing.

"Where do we go?" Elliott asked, and Buster barked.

"Is that a dog?" Bull asked.

"Yeah. There's a story there that is going to take a little to explain… and the stop helped us, in a way. Yeah, Elliott and I are going to need a place to stay. I can go to a hotel again, but I think I also need a different car. They are going to have made this one by now after our little chase through part of Pittsburgh." Things were out of control, and he couldn't see them getting back to normal any time soon. Still, his main task was to keep Elliott safe, and he was going to do that to the very best he could.

"I can make some arrangements. Come right to the house, and I'll have you pull into the garage. Thankfully it's a slow day. Zach and I will make some phone calls, and then we'll have some dinner while we talk. This is getting worse all the time, and we have to get a handle on it soon."

"Can you call Harry? These papers are going to take someone with a real business and numbers kind of mind to figure out. We have a lot, but Elliott isn't sure what's here, and that isn't my strength either."

"I'll call him. You two just get here as quickly as you can, and if you have any trouble, call the police right away and keep going if at all possible. If things get really dicey, draw as much attention to yourselves as you can if you have to. I hope it doesn't come to that, but get here and we'll figure out where to go from here. Call if you need anything—I'll have my phone with me at all times."

He ended the call, and Salvatore sped up. He didn't want to be stopped by the police, so he maintained a safe speed, but willed each and every mile they passed to go faster and faster.

Elliott couldn't sit still for the last hour. He kept turning to look behind them, and Salvatore watched each on-ramp for some sort of threat. Thankfully, nothing materialized, and they took the exit at I-83 and headed north up into Camp Hill to Bull and Zach's house.

The garage door rose almost as soon as they pulled into the drive, and Salvatore drove right inside. The door lowered behind them, and Salvatore got out while Elliott put a leash on Buster and got him out of the car.

"You have a dog?" Zach asked as he hurried up to Elliott and hugged him. Salvatore had to stifle the growl that welled up in his throat. "Come on. Take him out back for a while, and then we can all go inside." Elliott and Zach went through the back garage door, and Salvatore greeted Bull and went inside behind him.

"A dog? You stopped for a dog?" Bull's tone was gruff, and that sent Salvatore's defenses rising.

"He's Elliott's dog, and he's been staying with a friend, who it seems has been in contact with Elliott's stepfather. He put a tracking device in with the dog's things. I sent them on a wild goose chase. The thing is that the dog could have been used against him. Now Buster can't."

"Shit," Bull mumbled. "This asshole is like some damned octopus with tentacles extending everywhere. I called a few contacts, and they warned me to tread lightly. It seems that influence is being asserted at multiple levels."

"Then Losquaro is scared shitless," Salvatore said, and Bull nodded his agreement as Zach and Elliott came inside with Buster.

"What are you talking about?" Zach demanded in that light way he had that seemed to get to the heart of things. "If I know Bull, he's been giving you a hard time about this little guy." He bent down and petted Buster, who soaked up the attention. "Don't be such a mudge," Zach told Bull. "Harry will be here in a few minutes, and then we can look at the papers." Zach took them and set the folders on the table. "You have to be starved, and I have some pasta that I'm going to heat up." Zach left the room, and Salvatore's head spun a little.

"It's okay, he does that to everyone," Salvatore whispered as they sat down. "Just go with the flow. Zach always runs at a million miles an hour. It's what makes him special." Elliott leaned against his shoulder as Buster jumped up, settling between them with a yawn, resting his head on Elliott's knee.

"What's our next move?" Salvatore asked Bull, taking Elliott's hand. "We have to get this to stop. There have been way too many close calls, and one of these times we're going to be too late." The thought scared him half to death.

"We need to see what we have and then make contact with Antonio Losquaro. Let him know what we know and what will happen if he should so much as look at Elliott cross-eyed. The thing is that we have to make it so hurting Elliott will cost him a lot more than leaving him alone. But we can't do that until we know the kind of hand we're holding." Bull leaned forward. "Elliott, do you think he'll respond to reason?"

Elliott shrugged. "I don't know. I mean, he has a huge ego and doesn't like anyone to get the better of him, so giving up isn't in his nature. He just keeps wearing you down until you give up or make a mistake he can exploit." He sounded tired, and Salvatore put his arm around his shoulders. "But yet, if something is going to do him harm, I would think his sense of self-preservation would kick in."

"Whatever we do has to be decisive, and it has to come with real consequences for him." Salvatore wished he could make all of this go away for Elliott. Then the two of them could have a real chance to spend time together that didn't come with danger stalking them around each and every corner.

"I agree." The bell rang, and Bull got up to answer it. Spook and Jeremy arrived, along with Harry and Tristan. Zach called everyone into the dining room, and they sat down with huge bowls of pasta, salad, and a plate of garlic bread.

"Everyone eat. We can't plot the demise of a dickhead on empty stomachs." Zach took his place, and Buster settled on the floor between his and Elliott's chair. He didn't beg or even seem interested in what was on the table.

"He knows he'll get his later," Elliott told him. "I didn't want him begging and watching everyone eat and he knows it." Elliott took small portions of the food and ate slowly, while Salvatore's appetite seemed to have really kicked in.

"I understand you met Salvatore's mother," Zach said to Elliott.

"I did. She was a really nice lady. Forceful and knows her mind." Elliott smiled. "I liked her." His eyes sparkled with mischief for the first time that day, and Salvatore figured he knew what was coming. "She has the cutest nickname for him, though I suspect if anyone else tried to use it, they might lose a few teeth." He bumped his shoulder.

"I bet you got called a few names when you were in school," Jeremy said. "But once you got big, they stopped."

"Yeah," Salvatore said, and swallowed.

"His mom is really small and kind of petite. A real firecracker." Elliott grinned. "I would never have picked her out as his mother, except they have the same eyes and the same strong face. Other than that…."

"She got all the brains too… and she kept them," Salvatore said.

"I wouldn't say that. You're really smart, and you're funny, and…." Elliott's words trailed off, and he turned away, his cheeks reddening. There was nothing to be embarrassed about, not in front of everyone here, and Salvatore squeezed Elliott's shoulder lightly to reassure him.

"Last night, did you stay in a hotel?" Harry asked.

Salvatore nodded. "I don't know what we're going to do tonight. I think that needs to be part of the plan. I want to be safe, but I'm getting kind of tired of this asshole dictating everything about Elliott's life. It's like he's winning, and I've never even seen the bastard. I like an enemy you can see, someone you can look in the eye and take the measure of."

"Of course you do—you're as big as a house and you intimidate everyone," Jeremy said. "Well, except Elliott. I bet he has you wrapped around his little finger." Jeremy giggled, but thankfully the others didn't pick it up and the teasing died. It wasn't really the time for it, and Jeremy went back to his dinner, with Spook whispering to him.

"You're right, he kind of does," Salvatore said, partly because he didn't want Jeremy to feel bad, as well as letting Elliott hear it.

"Sal…," Elliott said softly, bumping his shoulder lightly and then eating a little more.

"You need to keep up your strength," Salvatore whispered to Elliott. "I know you're nervous, but you need to eat. Otherwise you'll get sick."

Elliott took a few more bites and finished up what he'd taken. Salvatore was tempted to load up his plate the way his mother had done when he was a kid and she thought he wasn't eating enough, but he refrained. Elliott was an adult and didn't need him making decisions for him. There had already been plenty of people in Elliott's life doing that. Thankfully, Zach urged him to eat and passed the plate of pasta to Elliott, who took some more.

"What's the plan?" Harry asked Bull. "I can look over the paperwork that Elliott brought, but that's going to take some time."

"How much?" Elliott asked.

Harry shrugged. "I don't know. I'm not familiar with his businesses, so I'm going to have to see if what you brought paints a picture, and that will take hours, maybe days. It's hard to tell. There probably isn't a smoking gun unless he kept records of his illegal activities as well. It wouldn't surprise me if he did in some way, because he would need to know what he's done so he could keep things in order. It all depends on what you have."

Elliott nodded and took a few more bites before sitting back in his chair. "I would hate for all this to be for nothing." He paled and shook his head. "I probably should have just left and let him go on with whatever he was doing. But I couldn't. He's hurting people, lots of people."

"Then we'll figure it out," Harry said, turning to Bull. "What we really need is to know what the police think. They often have suspicions, and they would definitely be watching a big fish like Antonio Losquaro."

Bull nodded. "I know a few police officers, but they are here in town." He looked at the others. "Do any of you know any police officers in Pittsburgh who might help?" He received head shakes and little else. "Elliott, do you know anyone?"

"I don't think so," Elliott answered. "If I did, I don't think I could trust them. I mean, he got to one of my best friends. Who knows how far he's corrupted others?"

Harry pushed back his chair. "I want to look at what we have and see where we can begin." He went into the other room. Salvatore wondered if Elliott would go with him, but he sat still, other than his hand gently stroking Buster's head.

"Let me make a few calls," Spook said softly. "I don't know if I can find someone who might know anything, but I'll try. I also need to contact Carson to see if he knows anything and to make sure there was no serious blowback onto him for what he did for us." Spook got up from the table and left the room. Bull followed, going in to join Harry.

"I'm sorry, guys," Elliott said softly. "I shouldn't have brought all this and dumped it on your shoulders."

"Yes, you should," Jeremy said, leaning over the table. "Spook, Bull, and Harry, they all need things like this every now and then." He looked to the others, who nodded.

"God, if Bull didn't have someone to protect or some puzzle to unravel, I swear he'd go completely apeshit and I would never get a moment's peace." Zach grinned. "It's part of who they are, especially Bull. When we met, he thought he wanted a quiet life…." Zach snickered. "That didn't last very long. Spook is the same way. They both lived lives of action and high drama for a long time. You don't just give that up."

"But I'm putting you all in danger."

"It's happened before, and I suspect it will happen again," Zach said. "But I think the one who really needs to be afraid is your stepfather. I can tell you that I wouldn't want to be on the opposite side of these guys. They know what they're doing." Zach's eyes sparkled with pride and sheer love.

"And all I was looking for was a job," Elliott said quietly.

Zach, Tristan, and Jeremy exchanged conspiratorial looks. "What you found was more than a job. We're a family." Zach came around the table and hugged Elliott from behind. Then he hugged Salvatore as well, before sitting back down.

"I wonder if there's anything I can do to help," Elliott said.

"There is. Let's clear the table and put the dishes away. Then I'll get out the cards." When Salvatore did a double take, Zach rolled his eyes. "When they get like this, it's best to stay out of their way."

"I'll make a pitcher of margaritas," Jeremy offered, and off they went with a burst of energy.

Salvatore helped with the dishes and then joined Spook as he came back inside. They went into the living room, where papers had been sorted all over the floor.

"Don't move too quickly," Harry said as he continued adding papers to piles.

Elliott came in and sat in the chair farthest away, Buster jumping into his lap. "What do we have so far?"

"A number of shipping invoices, some contracts, as well as the write-ups for real estate deals. Those seem pretty normal as far as I can see." Harry began laying out the shipping manifests. "All of these are shipments from either Canada or Mexico, and they're large shipments of pottery and coffee, whole semi loads."

"Do you think there's something wrong with them?" Salvatore asked.

"The manifests… no." Harry worked his way through another pile and handed him a purchase order. "This is what was bought versus what was shipped." He took the invoice and showed it to Elliott. "He shipped sixty large boxes and sixty pots. Only the pots are twelve inches high. It's likely there was something else in those cartons. That's the first one I've found."

"Should we try to match up others?" Salvatore asked, slipping onto the floor to try to match invoices to shipments. Elliott did the same, and soon they had paired up a number of others. It didn't take much for Salvatore to see the pattern. With each shipment, there seemed to be legitimate items, but they were shipped in oversize cartons. He'd like to know what was being included with them.

Elliott whooped and handed Harry an invoice. "Look at the delivery date on this one. It's next week. That means it's in transit. Whatever is in this truck is currently on the road on its way. The delivery location is one of Antonio's supposedly legitimate businesses. I bet they take delivery, unload the goods, sell the legitimate cargo in the store, and the rest gets passed on to Antonio's organization. It's simple, easy, and unless someone actually opens the cartons, they aren't going to be the wiser. I've seen these cases. They come strapped as well, so it's pretty evident if they've been tampered with."

Bull took the paperwork. "What I don't understand is if it's so evident to us, why wouldn't someone in authority pick up on it easily?"

Harry handed Bull another sheet. "Because this is the paperwork that goes with the shipment. See, it has all the same numbers on there, but instead of a single piece, each item is in dozens. So customs thinks each case contains a dozen items when it only has one in reality."

"And I bet that there's a man on the inside who makes sure that whatever gets tested or reviewed is the one case that isn't faked." Elliott sighed. "But what is he smuggling? The obvious answer is drugs, but all it takes is one damaged case and the scent is all over the place."

"Not if it's packed right," Bull interjected. "This isn't some fly-by-night group, but a well-coordinated business."

"It could be cash," Spook said. "Or any number of products. Drugs would be the most likely thing with the highest return. But people in shipping and at the borders are looking for drugs in everything that crosses the border. So whatever they are doing needs to be clever and damned good to pass through."

"These came through Canada," Elliott said. "And there are miles and miles of border that can be crossed quite easily."

"True," Bull said. "But the Canadians are just as vigilant about drugs as we are. They don't want that stuff in their country any more than we do…." He turned to the others. "Damn…."

"What?" Spook asked.

"What if it's drugs, but not the kind we're thinking of?" Bull turned to the others. "Many prescription drugs are a fraction of the cost in Canada or Mexico as compared to here. What if your stepfather is bringing in those types of things and selling them? They would be relatively easy to get, since they are legal… and some don't need a prescription there like they do here."

"Do you think so?" Salvatore asked, turning to Elliott, who shrugged.

"If that's what he's doing, then there would need to be plenty of money in it for him. Antonio doesn't do anything unless there's enough in it to line his greedy pockets." He smirked. "It sounds almost humanitarian to bring in medications that people need at cheaper prices, but the markup is only going into his pocket." He sighed. "Though I don't know. We're just guessing." Elliott got up and left the room.

Salvatore sat back as Elliott pulled out a chair and sat at the other table with the guys.

"Is he okay?" Bull asked.

"I don't know. I think this is really getting to him, and we need to bring this to an end as soon as we can."

Harry nodded and continued putting papers together. "I'm not getting any indication of what is in the trucks."

Bull pulled out details on the shipment in transit. "This looks like it will come across the border in Vermont, then to upstate New York." He grinned. "Which means the truck is going to come right down 81 and then onto the turnpike to Pittsburgh. It's the most direct route, and it's going to pass right around Carlisle to do that." Bull handed Spook the page. "Do you think you can hack the shipping company systems and find out where this truck is?"

"What do you want to do?" Spook asked.

"I'm thinking that if we can get the trucker to rest before entering the turnpike, we can check out the contents of his truck while he's on a break. Maybe figure out what's really going on."

Spook rubbed his hands together. "Let me see what I can do." He smirked. "And I talked to Carson. It seems that there isn't much interest in anyone going after Elliott. Apparently, he put the word out for Elliott. He said he can't guarantee that no one will take the offer, but it should help."

Salvatore checked on Elliott and then lowered his voice. "So why was someone waiting in my house last night?" This entire situation was becoming enough to give him a splitting headache. It seemed there were more moving pieces than he was able to keep track of.

"I don't know, but we're going to find out. I don't want to leave Jeremy alone, so he and I are going to come to your house tonight. I'm going to keep watch and intercept our visitor if and when he shows up again. But first I need to see if I can find out where our truck is." Spook snatched his bag from beside the chair and opened his laptop.

Salvatore let him do what he needed to and went to see what Elliott was up to.

"Full house," Elliott crowed as he walked in, raking the cookies out of the center of the table.

"That cleaned me out," Tristan said as he pushed back from the table. "Where did you learn to play poker?"

Elliott lowered his gaze. "It was the one thing the bastard ever taught me. I can beat even him most of the time. Of course, he cheats as much as he can, but I know all his tricks." Elliott divided his winnings back out and ate one of the Oreos that he'd won.

"You're playing for cookies?" Salvatore asked.

"Sure." Elliott raised his glass and drank some of the slushy green liquid. "These drinks are kicking my ass, so we figured it was better to play for cookies than money." He hiccupped and giggled.

"How many of those have you had?" Salvatore wondered if he was going to have to pour Elliott into bed when they got home.

"This is my third, and I think I've had enough." Elliott pushed the glass away. "I want to be buzzed, but not drunk." He stood and leaned forward, half falling into Salvatore's arms. "You know, you're really sexy." He smiled. "You should see what he has under his shirt. It's better and tastier than the drinks." Elliott slapped his hand over his mouth and giggled. "I need to stop. I say stupid shit when I drink."

"I see that… or hear that, as the case may be." Salvatore got Elliott back into his seat, went to the sink, and returned with a glass of water. "Eat some more of those cookies… or something." He wasn't angry, but Elliott getting drunk had not been part of his plans for the evening. Still, he couldn't blame him for wanting to dull some of the turmoil of the last week, at least for a little while.

Elliott drank the water and ate some more cookies as they dealt once again. Salvatore watched Elliott play, and it became apparent that he wasn't as intoxicated as he was pretending. Dang, he hadn't thought Elliott was that devious, but he supposed that when it came to poker for Oreos, there were no limits as to the things you used on your opponents.

After he raked in the next two pots on bluffs, Elliott sat back, grinning while the others all scowled at him.

"Maybe you need to drink more," Zach teased.

"I think you guys need to learn to bluff a lot better than you do," Elliott said. "You guys have more tells than Dear Abby." He pushed back the chair, and Buster put his front paws onto his legs, lapping at his face. It was clear that Buster wasn't going to be very far from Elliott, not that Salvatore could blame him. He wanted to be right next to Elliott as well.

"Got it," Spook said from the other room.

"What?" Elliott asked.

"One of your stepfather's trucks is going to pass through the area. They want to check it out if they can. Go ahead and play for a little while longer, but I suggest you find some other game." Salvatore patted Elliott on the shoulder and returned to where Spook was showing Bull his computer.

"The driver has been on the road all day, so he needs to pull off and rest. He's about half an hour out from the interchange, and I just sent him an email with a coupon for a free shower at one of the truck stops just off 81. My guess is that he'll stop there."

"Where did you get the coupon?"

"I found it online and reproduced it, then sent it to him. That company is in some serious need of a security upgrade." Spook logged out and closed his computer. "That's all I can do for now. In a few minutes, I'll check to see where his GPS has him located and we can swing into action."

"I'm going to stay here and work on these."

"I was thinking that Salvatore and Spook should go. Spook has the expertise to get in anywhere, and no one is going to mess with Salvatore."

"I'm going too," Elliott said from the doorway. "And don't tell me different. If my stepfather is messed up in something, I want to know what it is."

"El," Salvatore said gently.

"Don't give me that tone," Elliott snapped. "I know what it means. My mother used it all the time when she didn't want me to take riding lessons or anything else she was afraid of. It was usually prefaced with 'But you might get hurt' or 'What if something happens? I won't be able to live with myself.'" Damn, he even walked the walk. "Nope. I'm going."

Salvatore and Spook exchanged a look. "Fine," Salvatore said. "But you do what you're told, and you stay in the car."

Spook shook his head. "You can be the inside man. I have a picture of the driver from the company records. Once we know he's there, you can watch for him and signal when he comes out." Spook turned to him. "We are going to need eyes on the inside."

"But do what we say." Salvatore didn't like this one bit.

Elliott sighed. "Fine, I'll do what you say as long as it makes sense." He crossed his arms over his chest, and Spook laughed. Dammit, the dude laughed.

"You're going to have your hands full, just like the rest of us," Spook told Salvatore, then checked the time, booted up his computer, and smiled when he brought up the truck's GPS. "He's stopping. We had all better go, right now. I don't know how long he's going to stop, and if we're going to do this, it needs to be now." Spook closed his computer and put it back into his bag. Then he went into the other room and returned with a soft smile on his lips.

"Buster can stay here until you get back," Zach said.

Elliott knelt down, and Buster hurried over. Elliott loved on him for a few minutes and explained that he wasn't going to be gone for long. Buster wasn't buying it and whined at the front door when they left. Salvatore hoped it would be enough to get Elliott to go back inside, but he turned at the car, watching the door before getting in the back seat. "Let's get over there and find out what the hell is going on."

"Is he always bossy like that?" Spook asked, and damned if he didn't have a tilt to his lips that said he meant it in the dirtiest way possible.

"Most of the time, yeah." Salvatore closed his door and pulled on his seat belt just as Spook backed out of the drive and took off.

"And here I thought you drove fast," Elliott said as they flew down the freeway. Spook didn't slow down at the usual speed traps and reached the outskirts of Carlisle in record time, took the freeway off-ramp, turned into the truck stop parking area, and headed around to where dozens of big rigs were parked.

"How do we find it?" Salvatore asked.

"Here's the truck number. We just have to look for it." Spook reached in back and handed Elliott the picture. "See if this guy is inside, and if he is, message us. We're going to check out these trucks and then see what we can find." Spook pulled to a stop. "You know what to do. Just watch and let us know if you see him and when he decides to leave." Spook continued around to the side of the building and let Elliott off. As Elliott walked toward the front door, Spook continued back around to where the trucks were, and they started looking.

"Wesley Trucking," Spook said, and it didn't take but five minutes before they'd located the truck.

Have you found him? Salvatore texted. *We have the truck.*

No, Elliott answered.

"Shit," Salvatore swore under his breath.

Wait, he's here. Eating in the restaurant with a bag on the seat next to him, Elliott texted, and Salvatore relayed the message to Spook.

"Keep watch, and I'll be back in a few minutes," Spook said, and Salvatore nodded, trying to find a place to stay out of the way and not look like he was watching. For the first time in years, he wished he hadn't quit smoking just after high school. He could light up near the building, and no one would think twice about him being there. It was a perfect way to stay hidden in plain sight. Nonsmokers ignored you and didn't get too close. Other smokers tended to see you and would maybe join you, but as soon as the cigarette was done, they moved on and didn't generally remember you at all.

Still, he stood and looked around as though he were waiting for someone, keeping an eye out for anyone coming out of the truck stop to head to their trucks. It seemed it was late enough that only a few trucks arrived, but mostly it looked like the drivers were settled, at least for now.

He's coming! Elliott sent.

Salvatore strode across the parking area and slipped into the shadow between the trucks and back to where Spook had the back door partly open. "He's on his way," he whispered.

"Dammit. There are so many packing layers," Spook said. "Try to stall him somehow."

Salvatore returned, trying to think of what he could say or do, short of knocking the guy out. As he approached the front of the truck, the man from the photograph rounded the side of the building, followed by Elliott.

"Sir," Elliott called, "is this yours?" He held out a wallet. "I found it on the seat inside and thought you might have been sitting there."

Salvatore stayed in the shadows, smiling. Elliott's hand twitched a little, but he was probably the only one to know how nervous Elliott was. Otherwise, his voice was steady and he made clear eye contact. Damn, that was the exact look Elliott had when he played poker.

"No. I have my wallet. You might want to go back inside and talk to one of the clerks. They can probably help you find the owner. Is there identification inside?"

Elliott opened it and nodded. "I didn't want to invade someone's privacy or anything. I'll take it back inside and see if they can find the owner."

Salvatore turned at a tap on his shoulder, and Spook tilted his head toward the back. They made a large circle around the other trucks back to the car and went around to the front of the truck stop, where Elliott got in back next to Salvatore.

"Did you find a wallet?" Salvatore said.

Elliott smiled. "I did. In my back pocket. I figured you needed some time, so I thought I could buy a few minutes. He was really helpful and nice enough. He could have been an ass and taken the wallet, saying it was his. But I had to take that chance. Did you get what you needed?"

Spook nodded as he made the turn onto the road. "I did." He tossed a bottle of pills to Elliott. "Those are a highly controlled substance here in the US, with a huge street value. I managed to open three individual boxes, and two of them were that and the third was different."

Elliott showed him the bottle, but Salvatore wasn't familiar with them.

"That one is an antipsychotic drug, and the other is a superstrength painkiller. Who the hell knows what else is in that shipment? I took pictures of the trailer markings and things. Now we need to get back and figure out our next action."

Elliott leaned forward. "Call the state police and DEA. Send them everything, including pictures of the drugs, the trailer numbers, and the invoices and paperwork that tie it to my stepfather," he said firmly.

"Okay," Spook said cautiously. "You realize that we could use this information to get him to back off big-time?"

Elliott nodded as Spook entered the freeway, driving more cautiously as they made their way back. "If I did that, then the only person I'd be helping was myself. My stepfather hurts people every single day. He doesn't care about anyone other than himself. He'll put a thousand people out on the street if he thinks he can make a dime doing it. He sent people to kill me, the asshole. He needs to be stopped." He crossed his arms over his chest, and this time Salvatore put an arm around his shoulders.

"Fucking hell," Salvatore swore under his breath even as his heart welled with pride. "I think the scared little bunny just disappeared."

Elliott snapped his head around. "Huh…? I'm terrified."

"Being scared doesn't mean you aren't brave. It's doing the right things regardless of how scared you are. *That* makes you brave."

Salvatore smiled and leaned closer. "And damn sexy." He lightly kissed Elliott behind the ear and felt a shiver run through him.

"Knock it off, guys," Spook said. "At least until we get you home and behind a bedroom door."

Elliott chuckled.

Salvatore sat back up but kept his arm around Elliott. "Are you sure about this?"

"Yes. In fact, I'm wondering if we should send this to the news media as well. My stepfather has a lot of interest and supporters because of the way he does business. But if the media is involved, some of that support is going to melt away pretty quickly."

Spook hummed softly. "I think we should contact the police and let them do their jobs. We can always alert the media if they don't do anything. The more action we take, the more focus that could blow back on you, especially if anyone gets wind of the source of the information."

"You need to be as safe as possible," Salvatore told Elliott. "I think contacting the authorities is a fine idea. We can do that as soon as we get back to Bull's and let them take it from there."

"I want this over with," Elliott breathed. "And I'm tired. Let someone else deal with him now." He sat back and closed his eyes, sighing softly.

Salvatore relaxed as well. He was a little worried for Elliott. He couldn't help wondering, once all this was over and his stepfather was truly out of the picture, if Elliott would go back to Pittsburgh or stay here. The two of them hadn't spoken about anything other than the here and now, and Salvatore had no idea how Elliott felt about anything long-term.

Salvatore desperately wanted to settle down and build a life for himself. All those years in the service had pretty much left him without a home. He finally felt like he might have one here, and the icing on the cake would be to have a family of his own as well. His mother would be thrilled, and Salvatore's pulse raced just a little more at the thought of Elliott staying and becoming part of his life. Damn it all, he couldn't bring it up, not with everything that was happening.

Elliott had been through so much, and as much as Salvatore wanted to ask Elliott what he wanted and what his plans were, he couldn't do that now. So all he could do was wait and see, and that was one of the fucking hardest things to do. Salvatore loved plans and knowing what to expect. But this was out of his control. He knew his own heart, but at the moment, he couldn't know Elliott's. And unknowns usually sucked.

By the time they arrived back to Bull's, Elliott was half asleep on his shoulder. It seemed that now that he'd made a decision about what he wanted, he felt lighter. Elliott was definitely more relaxed and appeared more comfortable with himself. His fidgeting had calmed.

"What did you find?" Bull asked when they went inside, Buster bounding over to greet them. Spook handed him the pill bottle. "I see. He could make a great deal of money with these, either by finding a legitimate distributor or on the black market, and these aren't nearly as high-profile as the opiates." Bull set down the bottles.

"Elliott wants to turn everything we have to the police," Salvatore said, and Bull turned to him.

"The bastard needs to be put out of business, permanently. Let him come after me if he wants, but he isn't going to be able to ruin innocent people's lives any longer." Elliott stood tall, and pride welled in Salvatore. Bull even smiled as Zach hurried in to hug Elliott, along with the others, who seemed to have continued their card game to pass the time.

"All right," Bull said. "Let's get everything together with images of all the documents. We can call the state police and FBI tip lines with the information using a burner phone that I have. It can't be traced back to any of us or even to this area. I got it last year as we came through New York on our way back from Europe, and it's clean and, so far, unused." Bull laid out the documents one by one and gathered all of the pertinent information. Then he made some calls and started sending text messages while everyone sat on the edges of their seats, listening to his side of the conversation.

"Yes. We obtained samples of what is in the truck, and no, we will not tell you how we did that," he said in the second call, just like the first. "I can send copies of faked shipping manifests, as well as the truck numbers and where it's heading. I won't give my name or anyone else involved in uncovering this, but I can provide a great deal of additional paperwork that will lead to Antonio Losquaro. Give me the address and it will be sent." He jotted down what they said. "It's up to you to take down this menace."

Salvatore waited, holding Elliott's hand as Bull grew quiet.

"Yes, you can call this number for questions, but we will do no more than that. We'd also appreciate a call regarding any resolution. … No. … We're concerned for our safety and that things are made right. He's hurting a great number of people." Bull ended the call, and Elliott leaned against Salvatore.

"Do you think they'll be able to get Antonio?"

Bull shrugged. "All we can do is hope, but it seems likely they'll take some action. We just have to wait and see."

"Then I think I'm going to take Elliott and Buster here home so we can try to get some rest." Salvatore was worn out, and it was getting late. The day had been nonstop, and with all the driving from one end of the state to another in the last few days, he was completely exhausted.

Spook got Jeremy, and the four of them said good night to the others.

"Change of plan. I'll head over first. You give me ten minutes or so to check things out. Then bring Jeremy, and we'll figure out what's going on there." Even Spook had lost some of his usual energy, but his eyes were as sharp as they ever were.

"Okay," Salvatore agreed, and handed Spook a key. Not that he needed it, but it might be quicker if he had one.

Spook talked quietly with Jeremy, and they shared a sweet kiss before Spook left.

"It seems like we could finally be coming to an end," Elliott said as he sank into a chair. "I didn't think this was even possible and was worried that I'd be running forever."

Salvatore didn't want to burst his bubble. He knew this was just another step in this battle, and that whatever happened to Antonio Losquaro and his shady business, this was far from over... at least for now.

CHAPTER 9

ELLIOTT WAS worn out and grateful that no one seemed to have returned to Salvatore's house. He hurried inside and thanked both Spook and Jeremy for making sure he was safe, then used the bathroom, closing the door. Elliott cleaned up and then went right to Salvatore's bedroom and sat on the edge of the bed. He didn't mean to be antisocial, but he had had just about all of the people time he could stand. His head ached and he was so tired.

It felt good to have decided to stop running and make a stand. It would have been so easy to just try to protect himself, but then his stepfather would be free to hurt hundreds more people in his quest for more and more money and power. He was aware that if this didn't work, his stepfather was going to come at him with everything he had and that Elliott was not going to survive that kind of onslaught. Up until now, Antonio had had others doing his dirty work, most likely as he went on with business. But if he managed to get out of this somehow, there wouldn't be a place for him to hide, no matter what. Elliott began to shake and clamped his eyes closed, taking a deep breath to keep his head from spinning. He had done the right thing—he knew that. But that didn't mean his good deed wouldn't go unpunished.

"Elliott," Salvatore said gently as he came in the room.

"Is everyone settled?"

"Yes. The house is quiet, and Spook is in the living room. Buster is sleeping on that blanket you put out for him on the sofa, and Jeremy is in the guest room. I was going to sit up for a while, but you should go to bed if you can." Salvatore came around and sat on the edge of the bed.

"I don't know if I can. There could be someone trying to get in the house to hurt all of us. And what if…?" Elliott gripped the edge of the bedding.

"That's what Spook and I are here for," Salvatore said, but Elliott shook his head.

"I don't want you to think that you have to be my protector all the time." He lowered his gaze. It was time that he learned to take care of himself. Maybe that had been the problem all along. His stepfather was an ass of epic proportions, but maybe Elliott wouldn't have been so scared and stayed as long as he had if he'd been willing to step away and stand on his own. It was too easy to stay and tell himself that he was there for his mom. Antonio's money was always there, and it was so simple to just take what he offered and not ask questions. "I have to be my own man. I can blame all the shit in my life on my stepfather and his assholeness, but the real blame is on me. I had choices, and for a long time, I didn't take them."

Salvatore took his hand. "Then be your own man. I like that. You made a huge decision, and like I said, it was sexy. And if I can actually say the word, kind of heroic. You made the decision for the greater good." Salvatore squeezed his hand.

"Just stay here with me," Elliott whispered, and Salvatore nodded.

"I'll be right back. I promise." He stood and left the room, closing the door quietly.

Elliott slipped off his clothes and climbed under the covers, trying to calm himself. He had done the right thing, and now he needed to know if those actions were going to be rewarded or not.

Salvatore returned a few minutes after he left, used the bathroom, and then joined him in bed. Elliott knew this wasn't a good time, but he needed Salvatore and he desperately wanted to forget and to feel alive. Elliott rolled over and slid closer to Salvatore, his heart pounding as he kissed him with everything he had.

"Are you sure?" Salvatore asked.

Elliott nodded, not wanting to talk. He was afraid that if he did, he wasn't going to be able to hold himself together, and he had to do that right now. Elliott's emotions were so close to the surface. So he held Salvatore, pushing him onto his back and losing himself in his strength and solidity.

"I'll give you whatever you want." Salvatore's arms wound around his back, holding Elliott tightly.

"I just need you," he managed to say, and Salvatore stroked his back, sliding his hands down to his butt, cradling him and kissing him.

"What I think you desire is to feel safe," Salvatore said.

"I do when I'm with you," Elliott told him from the heart. He might not have known Salvatore for very long, but the big man made him feel safe, and not just because of his size. It was his heart, which Elliott swore he could feel beating under him.

A soft knock pulled Elliott out of his head, and he stilled, rolled off Salvatore, and slipped under the covers.

"There's someone out front," Spook said.

Salvatore got out of the bed, pulling on his shoes quickly. "Get dressed and stay in here. If things get out of hand, go out that window right there. It opens to the side and there's no screen. Go to the neighbors and bang on their door like the hounds of hell are after you." Salvatore kissed him hard and fast. "Please do what you need to in order to stay safe."

"But what about you?" Elliott asked, wanting to go through that window and somehow drag Salvatore to safety behind him.

"I'll be fine. Just stay safe. I can do anything if I know you're okay." Salvatore left the room before Elliott could find his voice again. Because damn… just damn… that said so much.

Elliott got dressed and sat on the floor on the far side of the bed, listening for any sound from outside. A siren sounded in the distance, and yet he heard nothing from outside the door. He was tempted to open the door to see if he could hear anything, but as time passed, all he got was quiet.

Who in the hell would have thought the sound of silence could be so unnerving? He fidgeted and tried to hear anything. Spook had said that there was someone outside, but that didn't mean they were here for….

144

"What the hell?" Salvatore said loudly as Buster barked. "You could have fucking called instead of stalking the hell outside my house." He sounded angry, and Elliott went to the door and cracked it open to find Salvatore being crushed by a guy in fatigues.

He bounded out of the room, raced forward, jumped onto the man's back, and put his arms around the guy's neck. "You leave my boyfriend alone!" he shouted, tightening his grip. Within seconds, Elliott flew through the air and ended up on the sofa, bouncing twice before he tried to get up.

"It's okay," Salvatore said, and the words finally got through to him.

"It's okay that this asshole broke into the house? Maybe it's okay if he kills me?" Elliott could only see red.

"Sal, where did you find the spitfire?" the man asked in a deeply resonant voice. "I hope I didn't hurt you, but I couldn't let you choke me."

Salvatore helped him up. "This bonehead is Tartus. Yes, that's his real last name. You can call him Bobby."

Elliott took Salvatore's hand, glaring at the much bigger man, shaking his head. "You know this guy?" he said as he put his hands on his hips, then soothed Buster. "What the hell were you doing sneaking around the house at this time of night? What the hell is wrong with you? You just about scared the shit out of me, and I have had enough of being scared. You're lucky I didn't hurt you."

Tartus snorted.

"What if I'd had a bat or something? I could have beaten your brains out. Not as though that would be bad, but think of the mess." Elliott was furious.

"Okay, little dude." Tartus put his hands up.

"I'm not little." Elliott was getting beyond pissed with this guy. "What's wrong with him?" he asked Salvatore.

"I've been asking myself that same question for years," Salvatore answered lightly. "So why are you here, and did you stop by yesterday?" He narrowed his gaze.

"Yeah. No one was here, so I let myself in and waited for you. But then no one came, and I work nights, so I thought I would stop by tonight on my way. I wasn't sure you were home, but then I saw someone moving around in the dark, so… maybe you were being robbed and…."

"You don't have a phone? You could have called. You scared us all half to death."

Spook patted Salvatore on the shoulder. "If it's okay, I'm going to go join Jeremy, and you guys can sort this out. I don't think you need me any longer." Spook left the room, and Elliott still glared at Tartus.

"So, Bobby, about this phone thing…."

"I lost my old one and didn't have the number, but I remembered your address from the letters you sent, so I came by."

"What kind of person breaks into a friend's house?" Elliott asked.

"I had a key," Tartus said, and Elliott rolled his eyes. This was quickly becoming farce, and he had had more than enough of it.

"Next time, use the damned internet to look up the number. That's what it's there for," Salvatore said, motioning to a chair. "It's late, and we've had some very trying days lately. We all need to get some sleep because we have lots ahead of us, including working late tomorrow night."

"Okay. I didn't mean to cause trouble."

"How about we get together next week and we can have dinner and catch up." Salvatore opened the drawer in the coffee table and wrote down his number. "I have your number, and this is mine. Put it in your phone, and I'll call you in a few days."

"Sure," Tartus said, and Elliott could tell he felt like he was being brushed off.

"He'll call, and maybe you can make up for scaring the hell out of me with dinner and some war stories or something." Elliott smiled, and damned if the big lug's expression didn't brighten a little. "You have a good night." He opened the door, and Salvatore promised once again that he would indeed call, and Tartus left the house. Elliott waited until he was out of sight before closing the door and jumping into Salvatore's arms, his legs wrapping around his waist. "Take me to bed." He rested his head on Salvatore's beefy shoulder and let him carry him out of the living room and back to the bedroom.

Salvatore's hands cradled his butt, and Elliott moaned softly as they passed into the bedroom. Salvatore kicked the door shut before laying him back on the mattress. "Someone is wearing way too many clothes."

"Make that two someones," Elliott said, and nimbly began pulling Salvatore's shirt up and over his head. Damn, he was sexy as all hell, and Elliott got his own shirt off as Salvatore slipped off first his own pants and then went to work on Elliott's. It wasn't long before they were both naked, with Salvatore leaning over him and Elliott pressing upward for as much contact as possible.

God, he needed all of Salvatore that he could get. Elliott practically devoured his mouth and held him around the neck as tightly as he dared. They needed to be quiet, but Elliott wasn't sure that was possible, not now. No matter what happened down the road, he wanted all of Salvatore, and Elliott fully intended to take whatever Salvatore was willing to give. At the moment, that seemed to entail a great deal of touching and stroking, which only increased the heat that was nearly driving Elliott completely out of his mind.

"We shouldn't let our guard down," Salvatore said weakly.

Elliott pulled him into another kiss. He was becoming addicted to the feel of Salvatore's weight on top of him, and he wrapped his legs around his waist once again, holding Salvatore tightly. Salvatore might be right, but Elliott was relieved that whoever had been in the house hadn't been sent by his stepfather, and quite frankly, being on edge all the time was getting to him. He needed to feel safe, and Salvatore did that.

Elliott groaned as Salvatore lifted him farther up on the mattress, his hands kneading Elliott's buttcheeks. God, it felt good to be touched, to be held and cared for. He had spent so much time on edge and afraid, and he didn't want to do that any longer. Elliott desperately needed to be able to feel anything other than fear, and as

Salvatore pulled back, his hands roaming slowly over his chest and then down his belly before reversing course, that made him forget the rest. Soothing, caring caresses that sent him floating were all he could think about. Just like during the massage days earlier, Elliott was able to let go and just breathe and be, comfortable in Salvatore's ministrations.

He trusted him. It surprised Elliott how much, but it was so easy—maybe too damned easy—to just let go with Salvatore.

Elliott closed his eyes as Salvatore's hands moved slower, creating trails of heat and longing along his skin. "Sal...." Elliott groaned as one of Salvatore's thumbs slowly circled a nipple, followed by a tongue that seared into him. He arched forward for more pressure as Salvatore sucked at his bud, groaning and trying to stay quiet so he didn't disturb the others but finding it hard to keep in the sounds.

Salvatore pulled everything out of him, and Elliott found it impossible to keep it inside, so he stopped trying. He ran his fingers through Salvatore's silky hair, thrusting his hips forward in unabashed need that grew more intense by the second. Then everything stopped. Elliott blinked and met Salvatore's gaze as his lips drew closer. Salvatore tugged him upward, hugging him tightly, his lips growing slowly closer. Elliott parted his own, and Salvatore kissed him, the most intensely passionate kiss of his life. It seemed like Salvatore had put all of himself into that kiss, and it damned near short-circuited his brain. The wrinkles in the sheet under him tickled, the softness only adding to the sense of safety, which allowed Elliott to give as much back to Salvatore as he could.

"Is all this so you can forget?" Salvatore whispered as he pulled back.

Elliott shook his head. "No. It's so I can remember." He closed the distance between them. "I want to remember what it feels like to be truly alive and to hold my own life in my hands." He smoothed his hands along Salvatore's rough cheeks and then up to his hair, gripping the strands slightly. "I want to know what it's like to have someone in my life who likes me for me and isn't interested in controlling me or having me under their thumb." He drew closer. This was way too heavy a conversation for this moment, and Elliott didn't want to spoil anything. "I want you."

Salvatore held just far enough away that Elliott wondered if he'd said something wrong. "Do you mean that?" He placed his hand in the center of Elliott's chest. "I can feel your heart."

Elliott sniffled as a lump instantly formed in his throat. "That's because you stole it." He bit his lower lip and placed his hands on Salvatore's chest. "Please don't ask for any more right now, okay?" He inhaled deeply and closed his eyes as a wave of vulnerability washed over him. He needed to keep things like that under control as best he could.

"Why?" Salvatore said. "I'm not going to treat you the way your stepfather did, and I won't abuse your trust or support anyone who does." Salvatore's gaze was as heated and sharp as a knife from the fire. "That sort of thing isn't love."

Dammit, just like that it seemed like Salvatore could see into his heart, feel what he felt, and he understood. "Love in my family is twisted and…." Elliott didn't even want to utter the words that came to mind in front of Salvatore in case they tainted him and this moment.

"You met my family…," Salvatore said, and Elliott nodded, drawing closer.

"I did, and I love your mom. She's amazing," Elliott said.

Salvatore chuckled and looked down between them. "Can we not talk about my mother at a time like this? It makes things want to go south…."

Elliott smirked slightly. "Then why don't we talk about how hard it's going to be for me not to scream while you're fucking me into oblivion." He pulled Salvatore down once again, cutting off more talk by putting their lips to much better use.

The energy between them, which had waned slightly, zoomed right back to high voltage. And damn, Elliott liked to be in control, but Salvatore's strength and surety had him giving that up to him. It was easy to put himself in Salvatore's hands—too easy. And he realized what that meant. He trusted Salvatore, cared for him… and yes, he loved him, even if Elliott wasn't ready to say the words yet.

"Why are you shaking?" Salvatore asked.

Elliott shook his head, trying to control the whirlwind of emotions swirling and churning in his head. "Because…." He opened his mouth and nothing came out. "It's hard to believe that what you say is real, and yet I know it is. I feel that you're true and honest in my heart. But my head is so used to being screwed with…."

"Then listen to your heart," Salvatore whispered. "Unlike your head, it isn't going to steer you wrong. What does your heart tell you?"

Elliott drew himself closer and kissed Salvatore with everything he had. His heart had been easy to read because he already knew the answer. It wanted Salvatore in a big way and spoke plenty loud and clear.

Salvatore groaned and held him in return, his lips tugging on Elliott's as their cocks slid past each other, sending a sweet frisson of desire racing through him. Even though he started it, Salvatore quickly took control of the kiss, his lips exploring as he rolled them on the bed. Elliott had more freedom of movement once he was on top, and he relished each and every touch. Salvatore seemed to have this thing for roving hands, and Elliott soaked it in, the heat winding up and down his back, everywhere Salvatore touched him.

"Dang," Elliott moaned softly. "I feel a little like a cat being stroked, and…."

"Oh, honey. You're no cat…," Salvatore whispered into his ear. "You're one hella hot man."

Elliott couldn't help smiling. "Where did that come from?" Those words sounded so strange coming out of Salvatore.

"I can be cool," Salvatore teased.

"I'd rather you were hot," Elliott retorted. "And you are." He placed his palms on Salvatore's chest, a finger circling his nipples. Salvatore hissed softly, and Elliott leaned forward to suck and lick on one of them until Salvatore shivered under him. He loved that he could make the huge, strong man quiver and shake under him. It was sexy as all get-out.

Elliott slid lower, trailing his lips over Salvatore's chest and down his flat, tight belly. Damn, he could practically get lost in the grooves he found there, his fingers tracing the deep indications of many hours of intense physical activity.

"You like those?" Salvatore crooned with a flex of his belly.

Elliott raised his gaze. "You know you're hot as hell." He ran his fingers over Salvatore's side just once, the muscles spasming a little, and Salvatore squirmed. "I know your weakness." And he loved how responsive Salvatore was to him. He had always figured that a huge guy like Salvatore would be stoic and all about body and muscle control. Salvatore was so intensely present and in ways vulnerable with him that it only added to his heart's intense draw to Salvatore.

"Tickling isn't nice." He chuckled slightly.

"Is this nice?" Elliott asked, cocking his eyebrows before sliding his lips slowly down Salvatore's cock.

"Yes…," Salvatore croaked, and Elliott took more of him as rich musk burst on his tongue. He wanted more, and from the way Salvatore's breathing intensified and grew shallower, more urgent, he did as well. Cupping Salvatore's balls in his hands, he massaged them while taking as much of him as he could. This was a challenge, because, like the rest of him, Salvatore was no small guy. Everything in proportion, and *fuck*, what proportions those were.

Elliott bobbed his head, using his lips to provide suction, and holy hell, Salvatore writhed on the bedding. He tasted so good, and Elliott wanted to make him feel as amazing as Salvatore made him feel.

"El…," Salvatore pleaded. "Please don't stop… I'm…." He gasped for breath. "So close…." He sounded desperate, and Elliott loved that, but he wasn't ready for this to be over. Elliott pulled back, and Salvatore groaned and gripped the bedding in his fists. "Man…."

Elliott leaned closer. "Can't have the show over before the main event." He reached to the bedside table and handed Salvatore one of the condoms, flashing him his best smirk.

Salvatore's eyes grew darker, and his hand shook a little as he took the foil packet. He hesitated, and Elliott wondered why, tilting his head slightly and waiting. "Do you...?" Salvatore handed the packet back.

Elliott blinked and took it, his hand the one now shaking. "Are you sure?" Elliott's entire body went on overdrive at the thought.

Salvatore nodded and reached to the nightstand, pulled open the drawer, and fumbled inside. Elliott chuckled and found the lube for him, showing Salvatore the bottle. Then he popped the top and put a dollop on his fingers. "Go slow—it's been a while," Salvatore whispered, and Elliott leaned closer, teasing Salvatore's opening with his slicked fingers as he kissed him.

The trust in Salvatore's eyes was nearly overwhelming, and when Elliott's hand shook a little, he steadied himself before pressing a digit into Salvatore. The heat and the pressure were incredible. Salvatore groaned, and Elliott continued slowly, finding the spot inside, and when Salvatore rolled his eyes, he pressed again. Salvatore quivered on the bedding, his cock bouncing against his belly.

Elliott made sure to take his time, and only when the soft sounds Salvatore made became more urgent and his eyes had become nearly black with desire did he know he was ready. Then he reached for the condom and rolled it on, got into position, leaned over Salvatore, and slowly pressed into him.

Elliott almost lost his nearly shredded control when the pressure surrounding him grew more intense by the second. It took everything Elliott had to hold back and not go too fast. God, he wanted this, wanted Salvatore, and the way he was laid out under him on the bed only tended to drive him forward. Only when Salvatore tapped his hip did he sink the final way into him. This was amazingly mind-blowing, and when Elliott slowly pulled back, they gasped in unison and Salvatore reached for him. Elliott leaned forward and rocked slowly, wanting to make sure that Salvatore had a chance to adjust and that he was ready. Judging by the way he moved along with him, Salvatore was more than ready, and he tugged Elliott a little closer just as Elliott's hips started to roll.

"Damn, this is going to be fast," Elliott breathed.

"Oh God, yes." Salvatore quivered under him, and when Elliott changed angles, he gasped, and Elliott sped up, instinct taking over as one leg shook, the excitement inside him needing to find an outlet.

Salvatore was stunningly gorgeous, laid back on the bed, eyes shining up at him, a light sheen of sweat sparkling in the glow that filtered around the edge of the curtains. Elliott saved that image to memory because it was something he wanted to keep and hold on to when things got tough, for the rest of his life.

"Elliott…," Salvatore whimpered as he stroked himself.

Elliott groaned and pushed Salvatore's hand away, wrapped his fingers around Salvatore's cock, and stroked him in time to his undulations. In a show of trust that held Elliott's heart, Salvatore raised his hands over his head to grip the headboard as he moved with him.

Elliott had never been so in sync with another person in his life. It was like he could read Salvatore's heart and mind and give him exactly what he needed. Salvatore's knuckles turned white as he held on, his cock throbbing and growing hotter in his hand. "I know you're so close."

"Yeah…." Salvatore's breathy words were filled with need.

Elliott felt the pressure building himself and slowed his speed just enough to hopefully prolong Salvatore by a few seconds. Then he tightened his grip, and Salvatore's cock throbbed in his hand, his release painting his chest as Elliott lost control of his own body, pushing forward hard and holding still as he spun into a mind-altering climax.

Neither of them seemed in a hurry to move, and when Elliott slipped out of Salvatore's body, he disposed of the condom and collapsed on the bed. He was barely aware of Salvatore cleaning up next to him, and then Salvatore rolled on his side, scooping him into his arms.

"Damn, that was intense."

"Uh-huh…," Elliott breathed, and slowly rolled over to kiss Salvatore without opening his eyes. "You're amazing." He nuzzled closer into his heat and let the happiness and contentment carry him into sleep. He refused to allow any thought of what the hell might be coming next to enter his mind, or what Salvatore really wanted Elliott's heart had settled on the big man, but....

He pushed the kernels of those thoughts away and just tried to sleep.

CHAPTER 10

A PHONE ringing pulled Salvatore out of his dream of Elliott and him swimming at a lake after dark, with Elliott climbing out on the dock, his bare, tight butt shining in the moonlight. "Make it stop," he moaned even as he opened his eyes and his mind reacted to the intrusion. "Elliott, it's your phone." For a second he wondered who might be calling him and if his stepfather had found him again.

Elliott must have gotten up at some point in the night, because Buster lay at their feet, curled into a ball. He raised his head and glared at Salvatore as though the phone was his fault.

"I'm getting it," Elliott said as he fumbled through his clothes and pulled out his phone. "Traynor?" Elliott said as he answered and listened. Salvatore sat up, growing concerned as Elliott's posture stiffened and his shoulders grew more and more tense by the second. Then, like letting loose a coiled rubber band, the tension snapped away. "You're kidding me. They went after him? That's what she said?" Elliott listened again and nodded, growing tense once more. "Thank you for letting me know. I'll call her." He paused again. "Buster is fine. He's right here, and I think he knows I'm on the phone to you." He petted Buster and thanked Traynor again before hanging up.

"What is it?" Salvatore asked.

"I'm not sure. Let's get dressed, and I can tell you and Spook at the same time." Elliott was already pulling on a pair of jeans and a T-shirt as Salvatore got out of bed.

Buster followed them out of the room, and Salvatore knocked on the guest room door. Spook opened it, peering through the crack. He nodded when he saw Salvatore's expression and then closed the door once more.

"I'll make some coffee," Salvatore said. He figured they were going to need it, and the rich scent had just begun to fill the room when Spook passed by the doorway.

"What happened?" Spook asked, and Salvatore joined them in the living room.

"My friend Traynor called. He was the one who kept Buster for me and, well, he felt really bad about what happened before." Elliott sighed. "He said that my mom called him and said that the police had been to the house with a warrant for my stepfather's arrest, but that he hadn't been home. Traynor said that she doesn't know where he is, but it seems that the authorities have a manhunt out for him."

"Do you believe him, or do you think he's playing us somehow?" Spook asked.

"I want to believe him. I mean, he said he was wrong and was crying. Said that he was played, and he should never have talked to him." Elliott hung his head. "That man has a way of getting to people, and if they seem impossible to break, he'll find a way, some leverage somewhere." He shivered, and Salvatore gathered him close as Buster jumped up and lay on the other side of him. "What I don't know is where he is."

"If the police have him in their sights now, they're going to be looking for him all over. Your stepfather isn't going to get away, not for very long," Spook said, probably trying to be reassuring, but his expression said something else. "This is almost over. We'll all need to be careful, but if you ask me, I think that anything Antonio Losquaro was involved in just became too hot for anyone to handle. No one is going to want to work for him and take the chance of getting drawn into whatever mess he's involved with. Word gets out fast." Spook sounded so reasonable.

"Okay. So the police are after my stepfather, and according to Traynor, my mom is trying to call me, but of course she doesn't have my number." Elliott looked to the rest of them. Salvatore knew his mother wasn't particularly reliable as far as keeping things to herself.

Spook pulled a phone out of his pack. "This is a number that I registered in California years ago. It will show the call coming in from Los Angeles. Call her on this, and once you're done talking, I'll remove the battery and then put the phone away for a while and I can block the number on top of it."

Elliott told Spook the number, and he dialed it and handed the phone to Elliott. "Mom?" he said questioningly, then lowered the phone, placing it on speaker. "I'm driving, so I have you on speaker." Dang, the lie was beautiful.

Salvatore leaned closer as he listened.

"The police are after Antonio, and I know all of this is your fault. I don't know what you did, but you need to make it right. You never liked him, and whatever you said to get them after him... you need to make it stop." Her frantic tone rang through like a bell, and Salvatore took Elliott's hand.

"What did they say they think he's doing?" Elliott asked, and Salvatore nodded to reassure him that playing dumb was the right thing to do.

"Like you don't know. Smuggling prescription drugs or something," she said.

Elliott looked to the others. Spook motioned to him, and Elliott muted the line.

"They wouldn't tell her at this point, especially if he's a fugitive. She had to have known already," Spook said. "They might have told her the charges, but they aren't going to go into detail in case they might want to call her in as well."

Elliott nodded and pressed the button again. "What do I know about his business? Antonio the asshole never had anything to do with me other than running my life and being a pain in the ass." He softened his tone. "What are you going to do, Mom?"

Salvatore nodded once again. Putting the emphasis back on her was a good thing.

"I don't know. He's gone...." Now the tears were starting, and it was pretty clear that Elliott was conflicted.

Spook leaned closer and muted the phone again. "She's playing you." He unmuted the phone.

"I know you took some papers from his office, but you need to get them back and make this go away." The hard edge returned.

"I don't know what you're talking about, and I'm not responsible for Antonio. If he did things that were wrong, then he can pay the price. There's nothing I can do about it." Elliott's gaze seemed stronger, and his shoulders squared. "I wasn't the one who married him, and now you have to deal with your own crap... as well as his. There isn't anything I can do." Elliott sat back. "I have to go now. But I'm okay, so don't worry about me." He pressed the End button, and Spook powered down the phone and pulled out the battery, then put it all away.

Elliott seemed to deflate right before him. "She knows what he's doing." He slowly lifted his gaze. "For the longest time I wanted to think that she wasn't involved and that he kept what he was doing from her. But she knows things...."

Spook leaned forward. "Elliott, she's probably an enabler. She likes her lifestyle and can't help hearing or seeing things, but she ignores them and makes excuses for him. Just about everyone like your stepfather has someone like her. It's sad, but I'm willing to bet that Antonio is manipulative and knows how to read just about everyone he meets. He got your mother under his thumb and thinking for him before everyone else even before he married her. I'm willing to bet."

Elliott nodded and seemed even more defeated. "You'd think my own mother would be more worried about me than about her husband the drug smuggler and God knows what else."

"She needs help, and I'm willing to bet that once she's out from under his influence and maybe gets some help, she might return to the person you knew before she married him... at least to a degree." Salvatore wanted to try to comfort him as much as he could.

"But maybe she won't," Elliott said.

Salvatore gathered him in his arms, holding Elliott tightly and trying to give him some time to adjust to the reality of the situation. Spook went back down the hall and into the bedroom, and the door closed softly. Salvatore sat where he was, rocking Elliott slowly, letting him grieve, at least in part, for what he thought he'd lost.

After a while, Elliott pulled away and wiped his eyes. "I'm sorry for acting like a baby. I knew this was a possibility, and I should have been prepared for it. But I can't help wondering what it says about me that my mother doesn't even care that much." He sniffed softly.

"It says nothing about you and everything about her as a mother. It's that simple, and has nothing to do with you. It never did. Your mom made her own decisions about what she'd ignore or accept. And she did that with no regard for you." An edge crept into his voice, and Salvatore realized how angry he was on Elliott's behalf.

"But what do I do?" Elliott asked.

Salvatore didn't try to provide a response, because there wasn't one. That question could only be answered by Elliott and no one else. "Whatever you decide, I'll be there for you."

"But you guys always have the answers. Or at least you seem to," Elliott said, half whining and maybe a little confused otherwise. "You all seem to know what you're doing, and shit like this doesn't happen to Bull and Spook."

"I bet it has," Salvatore said. "I've heard a few stories whispered through the club in a sort of reverent way. But it seems from what I can cobble together that about the time Bull and Zach met, Spook showed up with a beef and went after Bull. It was a little messy, but they worked stuff out. Bull always seems to be involved in something, from what I hear, though he tries to avoid it. Trouble isn't exclusive to one person or another. It visits all of us at some point." Salvatore sighed slightly.

"Did it visit you?" Elliott asked.

"Yeah. A week ago, this cute server at the club…." Salvatore winked and smirked at Elliott, trying to add a little levity. "No, seriously… I had more than my share of hardship when I was in the service. A lot of the heavier fighting had ended by the time I was in the hot zones, but I saw lots of people behaving badly to one another. A friend, a pretty close one, was killed, and a number of buddies were injured. Yet the next day I was back out on patrol." He didn't want to scare Elliott or bring up all the things he'd seen and done. Sometimes it was best not to talk about it too much. "I have some PTSD, but thankfully it isn't too bad."

"I see…." Elliott leaned closer. "Do you know your triggers?"

Salvatore smiled. "Yes. Weird things like the smell of an overdone steak from the mess hall. Those sorts of things can take me back pretty quickly, but I've learned what they are and generally I'm prepared for them. Mom helped me through a lot of it. She asked me what my triggers were and then exposed me to every single one in a controlled way. Believe it or not, it helped, though it killed her to overcook a steak…." Salvatore smiled.

"You had support and…." Elliott seemed to crumple again. "All the things I thought I might have had turned out to be air. *Pfffft*. Even a friend turned out…." He sighed once again.

"I learned to judge people by their actions and behavior. You learn who you can trust to have your back." Salvatore thought a second and made up his mind. "There was a guy, Jerry, in my unit. I didn't get along with him. Don't even know why, but the two of us just didn't see eye to eye on anything. I avoided him if I could. Not that he was hostile, just that I didn't get him and he made me feel sort of itchy."

"Did you like him?"

Salvatore shook his head. "Not in the way you mean. No. I just didn't get a read on him, and I don't think he did on me. Anyway, we were on patrol, and it was a beautiful, quiet day. Then just like that gunfire. We took cover, and I found myself on the wrong side of an enclosure, pressed up against a crumbling wall with like five inches of cover along the side. As I was figuring how to get my ass out of that hole, it was Jerry who came out shooting with everything he had and I raced around to the rest of the unit with him right behind me. He had my back all that time, and I'd never even known it." Salvatore nodded slowly.

"Did you become friends after that?" Elliott asked, and Salvatore pointed to one of the pictures on the wall.

"That's him and I right there, taken a few days later. He got a medal for what he did, and he deserved it. If Jerry would have judged me by the same standard that I judged him, I might not be alive. It turned out that Jerry was just quiet because he felt he talked funny, so he didn't say much and kept to himself. He had a slight lisp, that was all, but he had a heart as strong as anything." Salvatore turned away from the picture. He hoped to hell that Elliott didn't pursue this conversation any longer. The story didn't have a happy ending, and the last time he had seen Jerry was at his funeral. He'd made it home in one piece but died of cancer a year later. It still hurt like hell. "Anyway, I guess my point is—"

"I get it," Elliott said softly. "Love the people who are worthy of it." He took a deep breath and patted Salvatore's hand. "Maybe someday you can tell me the rest of that story." Elliott hugged Buster and then smoothed his head gently. "Do you need to go out?"

Elliott let Buster out the back, and he must have done his business fast because he was right back inside. They both joined him, and Elliott curled up on the sofa, with Buster right by his legs, and Salvatore found a light blanket for them. Then he sat in the living room chair, picked up the book he'd been working his way through for the last month, and sat quietly, pretending he was reading and not watching Elliott sleep.

After a while, he gave up on the reading and stretched out, closing his eyes, though his body was on alert and his hearing on point even as he dozed a little.

"I STILL don't think this is a good idea," Salvatore said that evening as he drove toward the club.

Elliott sat rigidly in the passenger seat. "I have to work." He had fussed before leaving to make sure that Buster was okay and had everything he needed. "We both can't go into hiding forever. And I need to do something normal, because the last few days have been some of the strangest of my life. With everyone around, no one is going to be able to get near me without someone in the club knowing

161

about it. I'll be fine." Elliott actually seemed determined as they rode into the club about four in the afternoon.

"As long as you promise to get one of us if you see or even think something is happening." Salvatore squeezed Elliott's hand, more than a little nervous. As far as they knew, Elliott's stepfather was still eluding the authorities, and as long as he was out there, then Elliott wasn't safe. The story had made the news in the area, and apparently a picture was being circulated. So as far as Salvatore was concerned, he'd be stupid to show up here, but Salvatore's concern was for Elliott. And he intended to keep a sharp eye on him tonight.

When they arrived, Salvatore backed into his parking space and locked the door once they got out and immediately headed inside.

"I heard what's been happening, and Spook told me about your mother," Bull said, and then he hugged Elliott. "You know we're here for you and have your back."

Elliott nodded and held Bull in return as a stab of jealousy hit Salvatore that he had to try to control. Elliott deserved all the comfort he could get right now. "Thank you. I just want to go to work and try to do something normal."

"I understand. But you need to keep yourself safe. All of us will be on the lookout, and it's a Tuesday, so things will be relatively quiet. But I want you to yell or scream at the top of your lungs if anything happens. One of us will be there in a flash."

"Antonio isn't going to come here. With all this heat, he's probably heading for the border with as much portable wealth as he can carry." Elliott stepped back from Bull. "At least that's what I'd do, and I know he has diamonds and other jewels that he had in essence put in his pockets."

Bull nodded, but his gaze swept over Elliott, as well as Salvatore and Spook. "That may be true, but I don't think your stepfather is going to see things that way. He is going to want his life back, and the easiest way for that to happen is for his accuser to disappear, one way or another. Spook said your mother blamed you."

"Yes." Whatever confidence Elliott had seemed to have disappeared.

"You can expect that she could be acting on his behalf." Bull pulled out two chairs and set one in place so Elliott could sit down.

Elliott nodded once again and lifted his gaze. "She has her own agenda, and I wish I could understand it. But you're right."

"Maybe not. I don't know for sure. I'm just saying that we don't know how Antonio is going to react, so we're going to take precautions until he's captured." Bull smiled, and Salvatore put his hands on Elliott's shoulders to reassure him. "Go on and get to work. We have some things to get done before patrons arrive."

Elliott stood, heading out to start lowering chairs and wiping down the tables. Salvatore got busy behind the bar, helping Hank get everything set up. He didn't really have any duties yet, so his job was pretty much to help the others until the doors opened. Then he stationed himself at the door, keeping an eagle eye on everyone who approached the club.

Of course, at opening, the few guys who showed up were easy to scout, but as the evening wore on, he had to keep a sharper eye out. There was no behavior out of the ordinary, though, just guys excited about the prospect of a night of drinking and maybe a little more. The usual.

"Anything?" Bull asked once it was dark.

"No. Just normal and sort of quiet," Salvatore answered. "Mostly it's guys we've seen before. Stuff like that. A few who tried to sneak in their own drink, but we stopped that."

"Okay. Go ahead and take a break for a little while. I'll handle the door for you."

"How's Elliott doing?" Salvatore asked.

Bull shook his head. "He's jumpy. Go take him somewhere and help him calm down a little. Maybe just let him sit somewhere quiet. Every time someone tries to get his attention or touches him, he nearly jumps to the ceiling. He hasn't spilled any drinks, but he just needs a little time to relax." Bull handled the next guys, and Salvatore ducked inside.

He found Elliott at the bar and got him aside. "Take a break when you can. I'll be by the office door, and we can sit and talk for a few minutes." He waited by the door and opened it for Elliott once he came over. As soon as it closed behind them, the thrumming beat from the floor cut off. Salvatore gently pulled Elliott into his arms, just holding him.

"This is harder than I thought it would be. Things I wouldn't think about before are bothering me, and I wanted to smack a customer for flirting." Elliott huffed softly. "I'm not sure how I'm going to make it through the rest of the night."

"Take a few deep breaths and just relax. That's why we came back here. It's safe and quiet, and it will give you a few minutes to catch your breath." Salvatore guided him to the small break room, where they sat down. "Do you want me to get you anything?"

"No. I'm not thirsty, and the thought of food is enough to have my stomach revolt on me." Elliott sighed and closed his eyes. "I keep wondering if Antonio is just around the corner or waiting to burst through the front door to come after me." At least Elliott's color seemed to be coming back and his hand had stopped shaking, which was good to see.

It wasn't hard for Salvatore to understand that kind of fear. He had lived it more than once in his life. Salvatore had seen what near terror could do, and he knew the strength that it took to live with it and go on. "I can tell you a bunch of things, but most of them will be just full of shit." He smiled, and Elliott turned to him and did the same. "But I will say this, and it isn't crap—strength is sometimes being able to go on, and a lot of the time it has to do with only one muscle." He gently placed his hand in the center of Elliott's chest. "That's the only one that matters. Everything else is the box that holds it."

"Mine feels like part of it is breaking," Elliott muttered, and Salvatore held him once again. "And I don't know what to do about it. I thought being occupied and acting normal would help, but I'm not acting normal and I don't want to be this way." They held each other, and Salvatore wished there was something he could say to make Elliott feel better. But what did you say to someone who had come to realize that the people who should love you most didn't?

"When we go visit my mom the next time, I'll tell her that she can mother you all she likes. Mom will cook for you and fuss over you until you can't stand it any longer." Salvatore waited until Elliott lifted his head. "Sometimes the family we're born with sucks."

"Yeah. That's true enough, I guess. But what do we do then?"

Salvatore met Elliott's gaze. "We make our own family."

Elliott chuckled, but there was no mirth in it. "I don't think I'd know where to start."

"You already have." Salvatore caressed Elliott's cheek, then held it in his hand. "There are plenty of people who care about you right here, and it starts with me. Okay?" Salvatore swallowed around the lump.

"What are you saying?" Elliott asked.

Salvatore hesitated and then found his voice once again. "I'm crappy when it comes to talking about my feelings. I spent years burying them deep down so I didn't go to pieces when I saw one of my friends get killed or hurt. I saw how that reached to my soul and threatened to kill it, so I turned part of myself off… or at least I tried to. If I talked about stuff, then it opened up again, so I didn't. And it became a habit. One I need to break." Salvatore took a deep breath, holding Elliott's incredible gaze. He could look into those eyes for the rest of his life. "I'm falling in love with you. It's as simple as that."

Elliott smiled slightly, and it brightened his expression, his eyes lighting a little. "I love you too. But I don't want this to be some protector kind of thing."

"It isn't. I can promise you that. Though I will say that protecting people is in my nature. So if it gets to be too much…."

Elliott rolled his eyes. "Don't worry, I'll put you in your place." He smirked, and Salvatore was grateful that some of Elliott's cheekiness was coming forward. Elliott checked his watch. "We still have a few minutes before my break is over. Do you want to make out or something?"

Salvatore got two bottles of water from the small refrigerator. "How about we leave that until we aren't at work?" He handed a bottle to Elliott. "Drink plenty, and then we can go back out there."

Elliott twisted off the top, drank a good share, and set the bottle aside. "I can't do anything about any of this," he said softly. "She made her decision a long time ago."

Salvatore patted Elliott's hand. "I know it doesn't soften the blow, but I don't think she ever actually made a decision. Your stepfather pulled her in and has probably manipulated her the entire time they have been married." Salvatore didn't know that for sure, but he thought that was a possibility, and if it made Elliott feel better…. "It's what people like Antonio Losquaro do. They suck people in at first, and once you're in, there's no way out again. Everything becomes twisted, like some alternate reality."

Elliott shrugged. "It doesn't mean it hurts any less."

"No, it doesn't." There was nothing Salvatore could say to argue with that. "Let's go back to work, and I'll keep an eye on the door. Bull is out front, and I'll stay inside where I can watch as well. I know it's hard, but try to relax. You have friends."

The music intruded on their peace for a second, and then it cut off again as Grant came inside. "I know you have a few minutes yet, but…." He seemed a little frazzled. "Both of you… please."

"Sure. We're on our way." Salvatore followed Grant and Elliott as they went back to the club floor, and he instantly made a sweep of the room to assess for any trouble. Elliott hurried back to his station and Salvatore kept an eye on him as he went into security mode.

"Is he yours?" a man in black jeans and a tight black T-shirt asked about an hour later as Salvatore was about to make a round of the club. "Because damn, if he isn't, that's one hot piece of ass." The man was looking right at Elliott.

Salvatore turned to the guy. "Yes. He's my boyfriend, and I'll thank you not to talk about him—or anyone here—like that. Respect."

"Please. He's adorable, and he must be something else when you get him home." The man grinned and turned so he once again looked to where Elliott was crossing to the bar. "Do the two of you play, because a few hours with him could—"

Salvatore cut him off. "That's enough. I think you've had enough to drink and that it's time for you to go home." He motioned toward the door.

"I don't think so," the guy retorted. "I just got here, and I want to have some fun." He didn't seem to understand that Salvatore was security for the club… and he didn't seem to care either.

"Actually, I do think so," Salvatore said more forcefully. He glanced around for some backup, but didn't see the other guys at the moment. Still, the guy hadn't actually done anything wrong, just talked a rather asshole game. "Club security, and you need to be more respectful to the guys who work here. Understand?"

The guy pulled his gaze away from the dance floor, his hands rising. "I'm not here to cause trouble." He backed away. "I'm not about to touch anyone who isn't interested."

"See that you don't." Salvatore made sure the guy knew he'd be watching. The guy was probably a loudmouth, and just because he'd made a crass crack about his boyfriend didn't mean he should kick him out. Though Salvatore did see Spook and pointed the guy out so that others could keep an eye on him as well.

The night continued on, and about midnight, Bull messaged for him to man the door. Salvatore made his way over as Bull came inside. A scuffle broke out toward the back of the club. Chairs scraped, and voices raised loudly enough to be heard over the music. People began moving away as Bull parted the crowd, and Salvatore hurried outside to secure the door and keep everyone calm.

The din from inside the club calmed as soon as he reached the doorway. He turned to where Spook and Bull seemed to have things under control before checking for anyone waiting or gathered outside. A single man strode up on the sidewalk, reaching for his wallet. As he got closer, he stopped, and Salvatore searched him to ensure he wasn't trying to sneak anything into the club. As he bent down, a cloth pressed over his nose. Salvatore tried to pull it away, but darkness tickled the edge of his consciousness. He managed to wrench himself to the right, throwing the guy off, getting a breath or two of fresh air. But it wasn't enough. The cloth was there again, and this time the blackness closed in on him much faster.

CHAPTER 11

ELLIOTT KEPT out of the way of the tussle at the club, which ended as quickly as it began, with Bull and Spook taking both men out of the club.

"Have you seen Salvatore?" Bull asked as Elliott passed by him. "He was supposed to be at the door."

"You know he'd never leave," Elliott said as a glacier took up residence in the pit of his stomach.

A young guy, maybe barely twenty-one, tapped Bull on the shoulder after coming inside. "Someone was out front pushing a guy into a car just a few seconds ago, and I don't think he was going willingly."

Elliott's legs nearly gave out as he tried to think of what he could do.

"What sort of car?"

"Black SUV, maybe an Escalade. It was big, and they took off fast."

Bull asked him more questions as Elliott's world seemed to shrink around him. He barely registered Spook taking his arm, leading him away across the floor. It wasn't until the music cut off that he realized where he was.

"Call him," Spook said, "and put the call on speaker." He closed the office door.

Elliott did as he asked, not expecting an answer. "Salvatore?" he asked when the call connected.

"Ahhh…." purred a voice that was way too damn familiar. "I see he is important to you. So maybe the two of us should talk about some things that you have of mine." He paused, and Elliott turned to Spook, who made rolling motions with his hands.

"I don't have anything of yours. I already told Mom that," Elliott said softly. "Is Salvatore okay? I want to talk to him."

"He's right here, but he's a little sleepy right now. Whether he wakes up or goes to sleep permanently is up to you. We'll meet you at

168

your friend's house, and you need to come alone. I'll know if you try anything." The line went dead, and Elliott put the phone in his pocket.

"What do we do?" Elliott asked. "We don't close for…." The beat that seemed to permeate the building grew quiet.

Spook pulled out his phone, typed something quickly, and then slipped it back into his pocket. "Bull is closing the club now. Thankfully it's pretty dead tonight. The doors will be locked up in a few minutes, and then he'll be back. I told him who's behind this." He sat down, and sure enough Bull came in and closed the office door.

"The guys are getting everyone out." He sat down, and Elliott relayed what little they knew.

"Spook, please get over there and as close to the house as you can. Let us know what's happening."

Spook nodded and left the office.

Elliott's stomach was tied in knots, and he jumped when Bull's phone rang and he answered it.

"What? … Okay. … Keep an eye on them." He hung up. "Spook says that the car is a block away and around the corner. He passed a black Escalade. He saw a man who looked like one of the guys in the club lighting a cigarette. I think they're probably waiting for you to leave so they can grab you too and get the hell out of town. I suspect that Antonio figures that both of you know too much, and he can't have that. I want you to stay here and—"

"No. I'm tired of sitting around and waiting for everyone else, and if things go badly, it's me he wants and I'm not going to let any of you get hurt." Elliott met Bull's stony gaze with equal resistance. "Call Spook and tell him that I'm going to leave and hurry out of the club as though I need to get to Salvatore, and when they make their move, you take them." It was simple, probably stupid, but all he could come up with.

"Fine. But give me a few minutes to get out there first." It was clear that Bull didn't like this, but he didn't offer any suggestions himself. "Then go out the front door and act panicked. That should put them off their game. But don't run." Bull patted his shoulder, opened the safe, pulled out a gun, and put it in the waistband of his pants. "Just hit the ground if anything happens. I'll message the police while I'm on the way."

"This needs to be over," Elliott said with more strength than he'd had in a while.

Bull nodded, then went out the back door and locked it behind him.

Elliott paced and hoped his courage didn't give out on him, counting in his head before leaving the area and heading for the main doors. Hank let him out with a concerned expression, and Elliott tried to calm his churning insides as he stepped out into the night.

Third Street was nearly deserted, with only a few others stepping out of the bars and the last restaurants that were still open that late. He turned and headed down the road, walking briskly and looking around. He wanted to seem like he was in a hurry to get where he needed to go.

"Elliott," Antonio snapped, and he stopped, turning toward the voice. "I knew you'd come running to help your little boyfriend here." The sneer on his lips told Elliott all he needed to know about how he felt about him. He stayed where he was, not coming close to where his stepfather stood.

"Where is Salvatore?" Elliott asked, even as he noticed the front of the Escalade parked a few cars away, barely visible.

"He's safe enough for now. But you need to come with me if you want him to remain that way." He stepped forward and yanked Elliott nearly off his feet and down the sidewalk toward the large SUV. Elliott managed to stay upright and followed. He had known this sort of thing would happen.

Antonio opened the back door of the Escalade and shoved Elliott inside, right on top of Salvatore. Elliott tried not to hurt him as he landed and then tapped Salvatore's cheek a few times to try to get him to come around. Salvatore might have moaned slightly, but he didn't wake.

The door slammed closed, and one of his stepfather's associates pointed a gun at him from the front seat. "I'll use this if you so much as fucking fart." He started the engine and backed out of the parking spot as sirens sounded, growing closer by the second. A pop from outside had Elliott throwing himself onto the floor of the back seat, and another followed, glass shattering and raining down on top of him.

The SUV backed out fast and then crashed to a stop, the rear of the vehicle smashing hard into another car. Elliott glanced up as his stepfather reached between the seats, a gun glistening in the light through the windows.

"No!" Elliott screamed and grabbed for his hand, pushing it upward as the gun went off. He held on as tightly as he could, wondering how long he could keep both himself and Salvatore safe, when the front passenger door snapped open.

"Don't move!"

Elliott didn't dare let go until his stepfather's hand relaxed. Then he took the gun and set it on the floor. Able to breathe again, he found that both front doors were open. The driver had been pulled from the SUV, lying on the concrete as his stepfather was doing the same on the other side of the car.

"Are you both all right?" Bull asked, once the back door opened.

"I am. I think Salvatore needs help." Elliott stroked his cheek just as Salvatore's eyes fluttered open.

"What the hell happened?" Salvatore asked, slowly sitting up. "Man, they gave me something…."

"Just relax. You were out for a while," Elliott said, wanting to throw himself at Salvatore, relieved that he was okay—that they both were.

Bull stepped back from the door, replaced by a policeman.

"Sir, we have EMTs on the way," the police officer said.

Salvatore nodded. "My head is clearing pretty quickly now." He blinked, and Elliott sat next to him on the black leather seat, holding Salvatore's hand.

"It's over now," Elliott breathed. "How much do you remember?"

Salvatore blinked. "Enough to know that a certain person put himself between me and a bullet. I came around as he shot through the roof. What the hell were you thinking?" Salvatore asked quietly.

"That if he shot you… I…." Damn it all, Elliott was seconds from tears.

Salvatore put an arm around him, and Elliott turned to Salvatore, closing his eyes and burying his face against him until he could get himself together.

"I feel the same way." Salvatore tightened his hold, and Elliott let himself be grateful that this was over, his stepfather had been apprehended, and he and Salvatore were both alive. He stayed where he was until EMTs arrived, and they took Salvatore to check him out.

Elliott spent the next half hour explaining what had been happening to the police, growing more and more tired by the second.

IT WAS nearly two in the morning before the police had everything they wanted from him. Salvatore seemed much more himself, and after promising that he wouldn't be alone, they released him. Spook never made an appearance, and Elliott had no idea what Bull had said to the police about what had happened, but they all managed to be released at the same time, with Elliott driving himself and Salvatore back to Salvatore's house.

"Are you going back to your apartment now that this is over?" Salvatore asked.

Elliott shrugged. "I guess. Though I know my landlord hates dogs." He pulled into the garage and lowered the door behind them. He'd figure something out with Buster.

"I have the spare room—you can move in there." Salvatore didn't move to get out of the car. "That is, if you want. You could make this—my house—your home. I mean, you could use that room if you wanted. I don't want to presume that you'd...." A flustered, insecure Salvatore was kind of cute.

Elliott leaned across and kissed him. "Why don't we discuss sleeping arrangements once we've both had a chance to shower, and we can do it naked, in your bed." He cocked his eyebrows, and Salvatore grinned. "Yes, if you're offering, I'll have my things packed and out of that apartment tomorrow. But I can't believe we're having this conversation in the car."

"I know, but it hit me that this is over and you…." Salvatore turned. "You're going to be able to go home now. You don't need to work in the club any longer. Your friends and the life you had before you came here, that's all opened up to you again. That small apartment and the life you have here that you built on the fly because you were hiding—you don't need that anymore. And I wanted you to know that you have choices."

"Yes," Elliott said softly. "I have choices. I can go home to Pittsburgh, where my mother and stepfather put themselves ahead of me and anything to do with me, and where my stepfather managed to corrupt one of my friends." He opened the door and got out of the car, because the air inside was growing warmer and he needed to breathe. Suddenly everything seemed to be closing in, and the relief he'd thought he would experience now that his stepfather was in custody hadn't materialized.

Salvatore had been so strong, so forceful and protective, through everything, and now he seemed so tentative that it was unnerving. He got out of the car as well, standing on the other side, and then came around. "I guess the question is, what do you want?"

"What does that matter?" Elliott asked more loudly than he intended. "It's never seemed to matter to anyone in the past. My mother does whatever she likes, and fuck all about me. My friends have their own agenda and call my stepfather when I get to town. What the fuck choice do I have about anything?" He shook and put his hands on the car to steady himself. Elliot didn't know where all this was coming from, but he felt out of control, like an ocean wave washing over him, knocking him down and rolling him along the bottom, and he was helpless to stop it.

"It matters to me," Salvatore said, and Elliott closed his eyes, doing his best to pull all the crap swirling through his head to a stop. "Why don't you tell me what you really want?" Salvatore slowly walked around the back of the car until he stood right next to Elliott. He seemed a little nervous himself, and Elliott's head was too crowded with overlapping thoughts to actually say anything at the moment.

Salvatore turned away and unlocked the door. Buster bounded out of the house, tail wagging, body winding around Elliott in a frantic display of happiness. Elliott petted, stroked, and hugged him before letting Buster go. He raced through the yard, chasing away some animal before doing his business and prancing back inside.

Elliott closed and locked the doors behind him, finding Salvatore in the living room sitting on one end of the sofa. "What do you want me to say?" Elliott asked as he slumped onto the sofa next to him.

"What you want?" Salvatore turned. "Don't worry what I want or what you think you can ask for, or even what you think is the nice thing to do. What is it that you really wish you could do?"

Elliott closed his eyes and sat still. "I want to stay here. I want to see how things work out between us. There's nothing in Pittsburgh for me any longer." He opened his eyes and turned to Salvatore. "I want to have Thanksgiving here in this house with you and your mom and Buster. I want a life, a real one. And the stupid thing is that I want a life here with the people who had my back."

Salvatore smiled. "Really?"

"Yes. I want you, but I don't know if I have a right to ask."

Salvatore closed the distance between them, placing his warm hands on Elliott's cheeks. "You haven't asked for anything that I don't want for you. See, I want you here, and I want to know what a life without all the chasing and fear will be like."

"But what if I'm too boring or…?" Elliott blinked. "These last few days—that isn't my life. I read and I sit around watching television. I'm not really all this exciting, and I don't want you to think you need to be my protector and all."

"I've told you before that isn't why. I fell in love with you through all that chasing. And think about it. Tonight, you were *my* protector. Hell, you were willing to try to stop a bullet for me." Salvatore sighed. "Why don't we agree to watch each other's backs?" He leaned closer and kissed him. "I think you're exactly who I've been looking for."

Elliott hugged Salvatore and somehow ended up sitting on his lap. There were definitely some advantages to dating a big man. "Me too. I certainly didn't expect to find someone to love when I left Pittsburgh."

"I don't think any of us intends to fall in love. I think, like with my mom and dad, that it just happens. Something changes in our lives and the right person is there." Salvatore brushed the hair away from Elliott's forehead. "There are times, I like to think, when life gives us things above and beyond anything that we ever expected. And for me, that's you." Salvatore's voice broke a little, and Elliott nodded. "I love you, Elliott."

Elliott hummed as he realized that the greatest things in life were those you never looked for. "I love you too, with all my heart." He met Salvatore in a kiss as Buster barked, adding his own happiness to the occasion.

Epilogue

Elliott hurried through the house that had been his home for over a year, with Buster right behind him. He needed to check that everything was just the way he wanted it.

"There's no need to be nervous," Salvatore said.

Elliott paused and laughed. That was true and he knew it. Josie was in the kitchen, cooking up a gourmet Thanksgiving feast, and Killinger, her husband of eight months, was helping. It seemed Killinger had many talents, including kitchen skills, and together he and Josie were having a ball.

"I just want everything to be nice." Elliott checked the dining room for the millionth time, the large table spread as far as it would go to accommodate fourteen people.

"It is," Salvatore said with a wide grin. "You've been planning this for days now, and it's perfect. The table is beautiful, and Mom's turkey is coming out perfect. These are our friends."

Elliott knew that, but these people had done so much for him that he wanted to do something nice in return.

The doorbell rang, and he jumped. "They're early. Can you get it? I need to put my shoes on." He hurried off to their bedroom, with Buster following Salvatore to the door. Buster knew that anyone arriving meant pets and scratches, and his dog was definitely an attention slut.

Elliott put on his shoes and checked himself in the mirror before joining the others. Spook and Jeremy, along with Hank and Grant, stood chatting, and Elliott exchanged hugs with each of them. Harry and Tristan arrived as well. The doorbell rang once again, and Elliott opened the door for their friends Angus and Kevin, hugged them both, and took the offered bottle of wine.

Josie and Killinger joined them, and Elliott made introductions all around before Salvatore popped open a bottle of champagne and passed out glasses.

"Bull and Zach will be here in a few minutes, but we should definitely get the holiday spirit flowing."

A timer went off in the kitchen, and Josie hurried away as the doorbell rang again. Elliott rushed over and pulled it open to Bull and Zach grinning, with Bull carrying a sleeping baby in a car seat. A boy, judging by the blue blanket. "This is a surprise," Elliott said, stepping back to hold the door open. Bull came inside with the baby and Zach with a huge diaper bag.

"We got a call yesterday morning from a friend in Social Services," Zach said as he set down the bag, and Elliott took their coats to hang them in the front closet. "Little Gregory needed a home, and I answered the phone."

Elliott knelt down to look at the little sweetheart, his eyes closed, feet kicking a little under his blanket. "Is it a permanent placement?" he asked, completely enthralled. He watched the little one sleep and then lifted his gaze to Salvatore. "Someday?" he asked, and Salvatore smiled.

"Yes," Josie answered from next to him. "Definitely yes." She bumped Salvatore, who nodded.

"It can be permanent if we want it to be. His mother is very sick and will never be able to care for him even if she survives. She has already signed away her rights, so...." Zach carefully lifted Gregory out of the carrier and placed him on his shoulder. "I think I'm going to be Daddy and Bull is going to be Papa." Zach snickered. "Papa Bull."

Salvatore handed Zach and Bull a glass of bubbly as Josie signaled that she needed help. Elliott hurried to the kitchen, following her orders as he helped with final preparations and carried food to the table.

"Dinner is ready," he said to the others, and they all came in to eat, little Gregory once again asleep in his carrier. Elliott put Salvatore at the end of the table with him to his right and Josie and Killinger across from him. The others took places as couples around the table. Elliott poured wine and refilled champagne glasses as needed before sitting once again, Salvatore taking his hand.

The house was filled with warmth. Slowly he surveyed the table as each couple took a moment to themselves. His friends were happy, and Elliott was over the moon.

Salvatore turned to him, his eyes gentle and soft, filled with love, and Elliott knew that no matter the twists and turns of the journey, they had all been worth it.

Salvatore lightly clinked his glass and lifted it without looking away. "To friends and our growing family, and everyone we're thankful for."

Elliott barely heard the clinks around the table as Salvatore kissed him.

ANDREW GREY is the author of more than one hundred works of Contemporary Gay Romantic fiction. After twenty-seven years in corporate America, he has now settled down in Central Pennsylvania with his husband, Dominic, and his laptop. An interesting ménage. Andrew grew up in western Michigan with a father who loved to tell stories and a mother who loved to read them. Since then he has lived throughout the country and traveled throughout the world. He is a recipient of the RWA Centennial Award, has a master's degree from the University of Wisconsin–Milwaukee, and now writes full-time. Andrew's hobbies include collecting antiques, gardening, and leaving his dirty dishes anywhere but in the sink (particularly when writing). He considers himself blessed with an accepting family, fantastic friends, and the world's most supportive and loving partner. Andrew currently lives in beautiful, historic Carlisle, Pennsylvania.

Email: andrewgrey@comcast.net
Website: www.andrewgreybooks.com

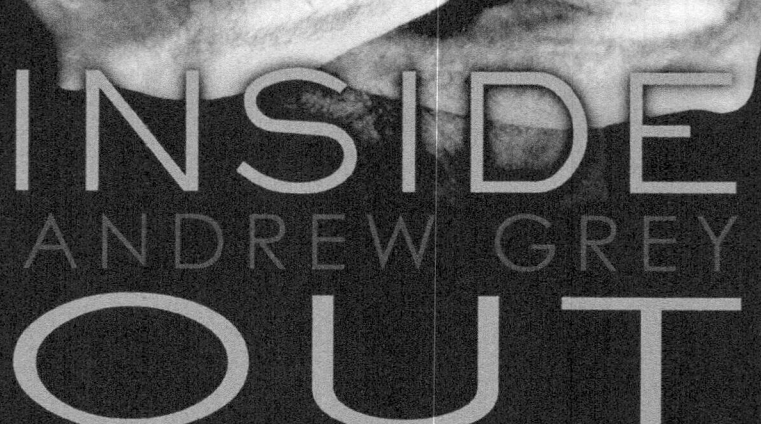

INSIDE
ANDREW GREY
OUT

Bronco's Boys: Book One

Former mercenary Bull Krebbs now heads up security at his nightclub in Harrisburg, PA. Working the door night after night, he's seen it all. Though tough on the outside, he's a little hurt that people find him unapproachable. Then he pulls a cute twink out of line to perform a random search, and he's surprised when the guy giggles and squirms.

Zach Spencer, graphic artist, twink, and seriously ticklish, isn't intimidated by Bull. He's in awe, and when Bull saves Zach from being trampled on the dance floor, Zach finds his inspiration for the superhero in his graphic novel.

Soon Zach wants more and makes his move by asking Bull on a date. Though small, he has a backbone of steel. He'll need it— their happily ever after is thwarted at every turn, including by Bull's interloping mother showing up unannounced and enemies from Bull's past threatening to pull him to the other side of the world.

www.dreamspinnerpress.com

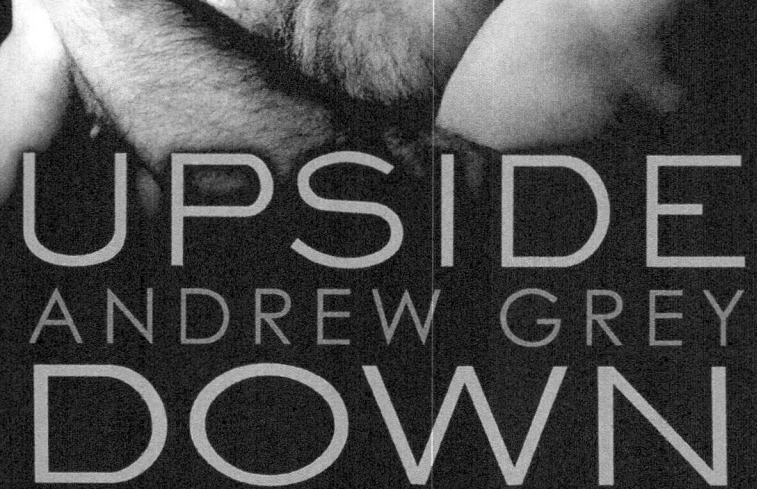

UPSIDE
ANDREW GREY
DOWN

Sequel to *Inside Out*
Bronco's Boys: Book Two

Lowell Cartwright's life as a mercenary problem solver has taken its toll, and after one more difficult job, he wants out. For help, he turns to Bull, a soldier of fortune turned club owner—not exactly a friend, but the best chance Lowell has. He visits Bull's club to scope it out and meets Jeremy Hodgson. The twink captures his attention in a big way. Bull tells Lowell to stay away from the club until he decides whether he can help, so Lowell stays in town. When he spots Jeremy passed out on the floor of a convenience store, he goes to Jeremy's aid.

Lowell piques Jeremy's interest immediately, pushing all the right buttons. Then, when Jeremy needs help, Lowell's kindness turns interest into something more.

But trouble comes knocking when Jeremy's place is bugged. Maybe Lowell's past is catching up to him, or maybe the danger centers on Jeremy's roommate Tristan's mysterious boyfriend. Whatever the source of the problem, the future Lowell and Jeremy hope for doesn't stand a chance unless they can find a way to protect themselves.

www.dreamspinnerpress.com

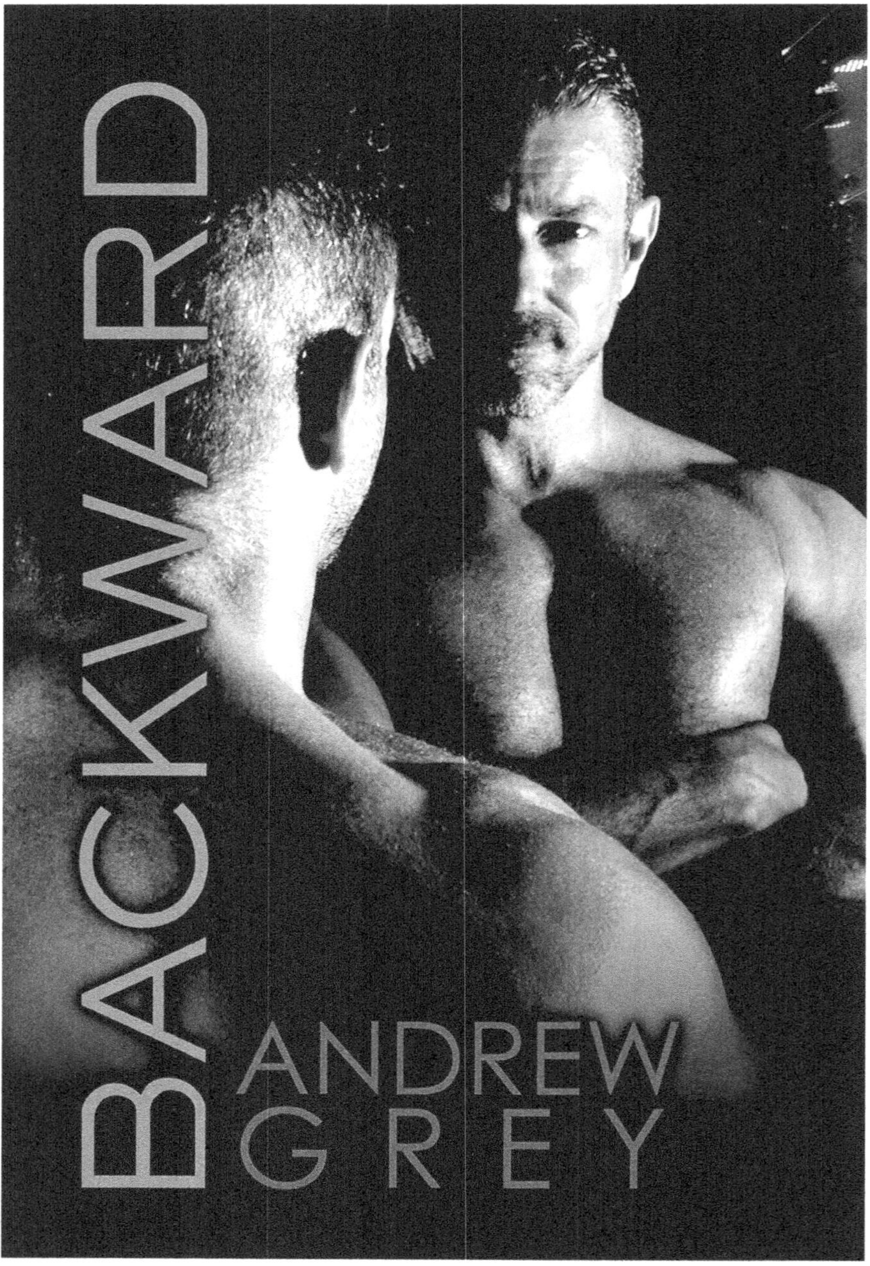
BACKWARD
ANDREW
GREY

Sequel to *Upside Down*
Bronco's Boys: Book Three

Club owner Harry Klinger has had his eye on Tristan Martin for months, but never had the nerve to approach him. He's watched as Tristan dated Eddie and then reluctantly sat on the sidelines during the emotional breakup when Tristan discovered Eddie was dealing drugs. Now that Tristan seems to be healing, Harry hopes to get his chance.

When Eddie sends his men into Harry's club to harass Tristan, Harry steps in to help. Tristan is reluctant at first since he admittedly has terrible taste in men, but Harry seems genuine, and Tristan can't help but think Harry's sexy as well and begins to hope for happiness for both of them.

Unfortunately, Eddie isn't behaving rationally, sampling too much of his own product. With his determination to take Tristan back, it'll take more than Harry's help to keep Tristan safe as Eddie ratchets up his attempts to get what he wants.

www.dreamspinnerpress.com

ROUND
AND
ROUND
ANDREW GREY

Sequel to *Backward*
Bronco's Boys: Book Four

When it comes to love, Kevin Foster can't seem to win. Some consider him a hero, but dousing an arsonist's attempt to burn Bronco's to the ground puts Kevin on the vengeful criminal's radar. Afterward, the arsonist fixates on Kevin, determined to burn away every part of Kevin's life.

Coming to Kevin's rescue more than once, and in more ways than one, is "MacDreamy Hotness"—firefighter Angus MacTavish. Not only is Angus smitten at first sight, he learns Kevin's nickname for him, intriguing him further.

When Angus discovers Kevin is the arsonist's target, he takes it upon himself to protect him at any cost. Soon Kevin works his way into a heart Angus thought he'd closed off for good. Things heat up between them, but the arsonist has no intention of letting Kevin finally find happiness. Hopefully Angus and Kevin can stop him before he reduces everything Kevin values to ash—including the love igniting between him and Angus.

www.dreamspinnerpress.com

OVER
AND
BACK
ANDREW GREY

Sequel to *Round and Round*
Bronco's Boys: Book Five

Opposites attract on an overseas holiday, but trouble has hitched a ride.

While Bronco's nightclub is closed for renovations, the owners invite the staff on a trip to Italy. Bartender Hank needs a roommate, and he's had his eye on waiter Grant for a while, even if he's had to keep his distance. But sharing such close proximity means sparks are sure to fly....

Grant has a problem saying no, and it's led him into some less-than-healthy relationships. While he's determined not to repeat his mistakes, it's clear Hank is different.

They're both willing to take it slow and explore the feelings building between them, but even in a foreign country, their pasts are catching up, and that could hurt more than just their budding romance.

www.dreamspinnerpress.com

Made in United States
Orlando, FL
22 March 2026

79557619R00115